THE ROMAN QUESTS
DEATH IN THE ARENA

Also by Caroline Lawrence

THE ROMAN QUESTS

DEATH IN THE ARENA

Caroline Lawrence

Orion
Children's Books

ORION CHILDREN'S BOOKS

First published in Great Britain in 2017
by Hodder and Stoughton

1 3 5 7 9 10 8 6 4 2

Text © Roman Mysteries Limited 2017
Map and illustrations copyright © Richard Russell Lawrence 2016, 2017

The moral rights of the author and illustrator have been asserted.

A CIP catalogue record for this book
is available from the British Library.

ISBN 978 1 5101 0030 5

Typeset by Input Data Services Ltd, Somerset

Printed and bound in Great Britain by Clays Ltd, St Ives plc

The paper and board used in this book are from well-managed forests
and other responsible sources.

MIX
Paper from
responsible sources
FSC® C104740
www.fsc.org

Orion Children's Books
An imprint of
Hachette Children's Group
Part of Hodder and Stoughton
Carmelite House
50 Victoria Embankment
London EC4Y 0DZ

An Hachette UK Company
www.hachette.co.uk

www.orionchildrensbooks.co.uk

For Emma Stringfellow and Dean Paton, who devoted a whole day to showing me Roman Chester, and also for Amanda Hart, inspirational director of the Corinium Museum in Cirencester

MAP OF BRITANNIA IN 95 AD

- - - route of the questers

CARVETII
VINDOLANDA
PARISI
BRIGANTES
EBORACUM
PETUARIA
DEVA
MAMUCIUM
DECEANGLI
LINDUM
CORNOVII
CORIELTAUVI
DUROBRIVAE
ICENI
ORDOVICI
VIROCONIUM
DUROVIGITUM
COMBROVETIUM
PENNOCRUVIUM
DUROLIPONTE
LACTODURUM
DEMETAE
MANDVESSEDUM
TRINOVANTES
VENONIS
SILURES
DOBUNNI
CATUVELLAUNI
CAMULODUNUM
GLEVUM
ISCA AUGUSTA
CORINIUM
VERULAMIUM
AQUAE
SULIS
LONDINIUM
SOFT
HILL
ATREBATES
RUTUPIAE
CANTIACI
BELGAE
REGNI
DUMNONII
DUROTRIGES
FISHBOURNE

Salve (hello)!

Welcome to the third Roman Quest.

This story takes place in the ancient Roman province of Britannia in the summer of 95 AD, during the reign of the Emperor Domitian.

None of the events in this story are true, but some of the places are real. You can still see Roman remains and ruins in *Corinium* (Cirencester), *Viroconium* (Wroxeter), *Deva* (Chester), *Mamucium* (Manchester), *Eboracum* (York) and *Camulodunum* (Colchester).

Most of the chapter headers are in Latin, and refer to something in that chapter. See if you can guess what the words mean. Then turn to page 231 to see if you were right.

Vale (farewell)!

Caroline

I

Chapter One
LUCUS

The night his sister Ursula fell from an ancient oak tree while cutting mistletoe with a golden sickle, Juba knew he had to get her away from the Druid academy.

It was late one evening near the end of June when Juba returned from a shopping expedition to the nearest town, Lactodurum. As the two white ponies pulled his chariot into the secret grove called Mistletoe Oak, he could hear chanting. He reined in the team and jumped down. Although it was nearly midnight, he could make out four figures standing beneath the ancient tree that gave Mistletoe Oak its name. Holding a white cloak stretched out between them, they were looking up and chanting, *'From air to us but not to earth, send your gift, O goddess.'*

Juba shivered. On a moonlit night like this, Britannia really did seem to be at the furthest edge of the world. It was hard to believe that less than a year ago he and Ursula and their older brother Fronto had been living in Rome in an opulent villa only a stone's throw from the Emperor's Palace.

He unhitched the two ponies and led them into the torch-lit tent. It served as stables for a team of black ponies as well as the whites, and also two oxen. He could brush and feed the ponies later, but he wanted to find out what strange rite the student Druids were performing.

'I'm sorry I'm late!' he called as he came out of the tent. 'One of the wheels came off and I had to find a blacksmith.'

The two boys and two girls stopped chanting and turned their heads. As Juba came closer he could make out their faces in the purple dusk. Unlike him, they were all Britons with pale skin.

'Where's my sister?' he asked.

'Up in the highest branches,' said a youth with dark red hair. 'She's gathering mistletoe according to the custom.' Although not yet fourteen, Prasutus had appointed himself their temporary teacher.

Juba frowned. He did not mind the Druid's philosophy of a peaceful life in harmony with nature, but he was deeply suspicious of any magic they attempted. Not only was sorcery illegal in the Roman Empire, it was dangerous.

From far up above, Juba heard his sister call down. 'Why have you all stopped chanting?'

'Your brother's back!' A pretty girl with copper-coloured hair laughed. 'You're in trouble now!' Bouda had befriended them in Londinium and offered to be their guide. The descendent of a warrior queen named Boudica, she was not at Mistletoe Oak to learn Druid ways, but to survive. Like Juba and Ursula, Bouda was hiding from men who wanted to hurt her.

Juba cupped his hands around his mouth to direct his voice upwards. 'Ursula! Why in Jupiter's name are you gathering mistletoe in the middle of the night?'

'The sprigs have to be gathered with a golden sickle under the light of a Druid moon!'

'What's a Druid moon?' Juba looked at the others.

4

Silver-blonde Bircha pointed up. 'That's a Druid moon,' she said. 'See how it looks like a capital letter D?'

'I suppose.'

'That's how you can tell it's a six-day-old moon!' said Bircha's older brother Bolianus. He had feathery brown hair and a nose like a hawk's beak. 'The D stands for Druid.'

'You mustn't let the mistletoe touch the ground,' Prasutus explained. 'That's why we're holding the cloak.'

As if on cue, a sprig of mistletoe tumbled down from the dark upper branches and landed softly in the middle of the cloak.

'*From air to us but not to earth, send your gift, O goddess,*' Bircha chanted. She reached out her right hand, gently grasped the mistletoe and put it carefully in a basket on the ground. 'That's eight!' she called up to Ursula. 'You only need one more!'

Juba frowned at Prasutus. 'Is this for another one of your potions?' he asked. A few months earlier, Ursula had drunk a potion that helped her hear what trees were saying. Juba knew he should have put a stop to it there and then.

'Yes,' said Prasutus. 'This potion will allow her to advance from Leaf level to Fur level and eventually to Feather level. Then she'll be able to fly!' His dark blue eyes gleamed in the moonlight.

'Fly? How will she fly?'

'The potion loosens her soul, so that she can send it into a bird and see through its eyes.'

Juba's jaw dropped. '*What?*' Like his Roman father, Juba observed the Stoic philosophy, which taught that the best life was achieved by avoiding extreme emotions, especially anger. He was having trouble controlling his anger now, so he took a deep breath.

'Ursula is very gifted,' said Prasutus. 'She achieved Leaf

level on her first attempt. Now she has to achieve Fur level by inhabiting a mouse, shrew or other small mammal. Then she can move on to Feather.'

Juba glared at him. 'How can you let her do that? I thought you Druids believed the human soul to be divine and immortal, as we Stoics do!'

'We do!'

'Then how can you even think of sending someone's soul into a shrew or a mouse? What if their soul gets trapped?' Juba realised he was shouting. He took a deep breath to calm himself.

'But Juba,' came Ursula's voice from high above, 'the risk is worth it if it means I'll be able to *fly*! Keep chanting!' she commanded the others. 'I have to get one more.'

'*From air to us but not to earth, send your gift, O goddess,*' they chanted.

The final sprig dropped onto the cloak and Bircha put it in the basket.

'*Send your gift, O goddess,*' echoed a harsh voice from one of the branches. It was Ursula's talking bird, Loquax.

From high above, Juba heard the ominous crack of a branch, and then his sister screamed.

Ursula was flying.

But not in a good way.

Chapter Two
CASUS

As Ursula fell from the highest branches of the lofty oak, time seemed to stretch out like a clump of sheep's wool pulled from a spindle.

She saw images from her life passing before her eyes, like frescoes on a wall.

The oldest images came first.

She saw her fair-skinned mother weaving at the loom and her dark-skinned father arranging gemstones on a piece of silk. She saw her old door-slave Cardo letting her toddle out of the villa and across a cobbled street to a spattering fountain. It was the first time she had realised there was a world outside her vast Roman townhouse.

She saw the faces of her older brothers Juba and Fronto looking up at her, for she was always climbing things. She saw the black bird that she later named Loquax flapping in the rose courtyard with a broken wing. And the wide-eyed face of her baby sister Dora.

Other pictures that flashed across the wall of her vision were less pleasant.

Fleeing their townhouse at midnight. Stopping for an abandoned kitten. Running in the necropolis of Ostia with the baby sister whom she would never hold again. She saw the linen sail of the ship that would take them away from Italy, and the life she had taken for granted.

She saw Castor, the beautiful Jewish boy who owned the merchant ship *Centaur*. He had saved her kitten from being washed overboard and later – weeks later – he had told her she was the bravest person he knew. She remembered falling in love with him at that moment, even though she was only nine and he not yet fourteen.

She saw the hundred different views from the top of the mast where she had spent most of the six-week sea voyage.

Then there was the terrifying storm at sea, and later her first glimpse of the white cliffs of Britannia.

She saw the dark and cramped tavern room in Londinium, with its tilted floor. The soldiers who arrested them at dawn and took them to a kind Roman lady named Flavia Gemina, who became their patroness and protector.

Ursula saw her rich and handsome uncle in his palatial villa on the south coast of Britannia. She saw the dozen fair-haired children, chained at the neck in a room of his Italian-type palace. The flight to safety through the marshes of a place called Fishbrook.

The joyful faces of the children's parents as they drove a fine ox-drawn carruca into the Belgae village called Soft Hill.

And now all the images came faster and faster, as if lit by flashes of lightning.

Herding geese.

Milking a goat.

Watching a lamb being born.

Grinding grain.

The village bard, lit by flickering hearth fire.

8

Fronto rising up from water, fully clothed.

Juba teaching Latin to the villagers.

A hooded figure in a chariot about to snatch her from a meadow.

Druid pupils sitting cross-legged beneath an ancient oak.

Bouda standing in a chariot, giving a speech to painted Briton warriors.

A man burning to death in a dark forest.

And, finally, Castor's identical twin Raven who had been raised in Britannia and wore the white cloak of a Druid.

That was the last thing she saw: a white cloak rushing up to meet her.

Chapter Three
PISTILLUM

'Pull the cloak tight!' cried Juba, grabbing an edge of the cloak. The five of them all took a step back, just in time. The cloth was pulled taut, but his sister struck with such force that their arms were yanked down and she hit the earth with a thump.

'Ursula!' Juba crouched beside her. 'Are you all right?'

For a terrible moment she lay utterly still.

Then she gasped and her eyelids fluttered.

'Thank the gods!' Juba breathed and then rounded on Prasutus. 'How could you let this happen?' he cried. 'You shouldn't let her run before she can walk. That's why I hate all this Druid magic!'

Prasutus did not reply. In the deep violet of twilight his face looked very pale. Juba noticed he was holding his sister's hand.

'*Meeer!*' A young cat moved stiffly forward and rubbed against Ursula's cheek, purring loudly.

Suddenly Ursula's eyes opened. 'Meer!'

'She's right here.' Prasutus squeezed her hand. 'She fell too, but she landed on her feet.'

Juba took his sister's other hand. 'Ursula, are you all right?'

Ursula blinked up at him. 'Raven?' she said.

'No, it's me, Juba. Raven went away last month.'

'I know that.' Ursula struggled to sit up, and they all helped her. She stroked Meer, who was rubbing up against her. 'I meant, is he back?'

'Not yet.'

'The mistletoe!' Ursula cried suddenly. 'Is the mistletoe all right?'

'Yes.' Bircha held up a basket. 'I have all nine sprigs here. None of them touched the ground.'

Juba scowled. 'I don't like this, Ursula. Not only is Druid magic illegal, but it's dangerous!'

'It's not dangerous!' Ursula brushed the stray tendril of black hair out of her eyes. 'And nobody will find us in this secret glade.'

'It *is* dangerous!' Juba insisted. 'Mistletoe is poisonous.'

His sister started to rise, but fell back. Juba and Prasutus caught her and helped her to her feet.

As Ursula took a tentative step, she winced. 'I'm only a little bruised,' she said. 'Thanks for catching me.' She turned to look at the basket full of mistletoe. 'May I have one of those sprigs? That nice one with the three berries?' She chose a sprig and limped towards a small round hut, followed by the others.

Juba sighed deeply. His sister was the most impulsive and stubborn person he knew. 'Dear Jupiter,' he prayed, 'give me wisdom.' Then he went after her.

When Juba entered the roundhouse, firelight showed them gathered around an oak table by one of the curved walls. Ursula was grinding something in the small marble mortar that they used for pepper. As he came closer, Juba saw Ursula put three mistletoe berries in the mortar along with some red moss, dried mushroom and mint leaves.

As she started to grind these ingredients to paste, the others

11

began to chant. Juba marvelled at how his ten-year-old sister had them all under her thrall.

In the flickering firelight, muttering her incantations as she ground pungent herbs, Ursula seemed like a young witch.

He continued to watch in horrified fascination as she added a dollop of honey from a ceramic pot and two splashes of vinegar from a square bottle of pale blue glass. Then she reached for a round jar with air holes in the side and a lid on top.

As she removed the lid, Juba heard squeaking from inside the pot.

Ursula reached in, pulled out a small black pellet and added it to the mixture.

'Is that mouse dung?' gasped Juba. 'Did you just put *mouse dung* in your potion?'

Ursula nodded and smiled. 'You have to put something of the host animal in,' she said. 'It should really be dried dung but I didn't have any of that. I only caught the mouse yesterday.'

'Add some more water,' advised Prasutus. 'And I think you should add some mugwort.'

Ursula nodded silently and added water from a jug and crushed leaves from a small clay jar.

'This is madness!' Juba turned to the boy who had appointed himself their teacher. In the light of the central hearth fire, Prasutus's hair was the dark red of iron fresh from the forge.

'Do you even know what you're doing?' Juba asked him. 'Doesn't it take twenty years to master the Druid arts? You're only thirteen years old!'

'I'm almost fourteen,' said Prasutus. 'And Raven was only thirteen the first time he took the potion.' But his eyebrows came together in a slight frown.

'Raven was raised by Snakebeard,' Bolianus reminded him.

'He studied Druid arts for a long time.'

'Didn't Raven tell us this spell was dangerous?' silver-blonde Bircha said to Prasutus.

Juba looked up sharply. 'Why?'

Prasutus's frown deepened. 'It's dangerous because you don't actually become the creature; your soul merely inhabits its body. If the creature dies while you are possessing it, your soul may not find its way back.'

Hawk-nosed Bolianus nodded. 'Remember the story Raven told us? About the girl who stayed in a deer too long and ended up in a speechless trance? The only thing she could do was beg by the side of the road.'

'Then for Jupiter's sake, Ursula, don't drink it!' cried Juba. 'I don't know why you're doing this anyway. You almost break your neck getting poison berries. Then you add evil-looking mushroom, bitter mugwort and mouse dung?' He shook his head in disbelief. 'This is witchcraft! You're trying to get power.'

Ursula stopped grinding the leaves and looked at him. Her cheeks were scratched by branches and an oak leaf was tangled in her silky black curls, but her grey-green eyes shone almost as brightly as the hearth fire.

'I don't care about power,' she said. 'I only want to FLY! And this is the first step.'

Then, to Juba's horror, she drank the potion down in five great gulps.

Chapter Four
MUS

Ursula almost gagged as she gulped down the bitter sludge of moss, mushrooms, mistletoe, mugwort and mouse dung.

Her whole body shuddered with revulsion as she put down the empty beaker. She must not think about what she had just drunk or she might vomit it all up again. She hadn't been lying when she told Juba she wanted to fly; it had always been one of her dearest dreams. But she also wanted to fly so that she could impress Raven, whom she loved even more than she loved his twin brother Castor.

Aware that the potion would soon take effect, Ursula picked up the mouse in his jar and limped out of the roundhouse and across the moonlit clearing towards the burrow in the hill where the Archdruid Snakebeard had lived. The small dark space was enclosed and she could send her spirit into the mouse, safe in the knowledge that nothing could happen to either of them in there. She did not want to spend the rest of her life begging by the side of the road.

Halfway across the moonlit glade, she stopped to look around at the night-time trees.

When she had first arrived in Britannia she had not even known the names of the trees.

But now, thanks to Raven, she knew not only their names, but their voices. Hazel had a mink voice: soft and silver-grey. Hawthorn spoke with a dozen voices at once. Holly had a voice as glossy and prickly as her leaves.

Even the thousand-year-old oak at the centre of the grove had once spoken to her in a deep gravelly voice that she felt in her breastbone. He had simply said: 'Ursula.'

And now she was about to ascend to a new level, where she could understand animals and birds. At the thought of it, a deep joy filled her, along with a deeper surge of love for the youth who had opened this world for her: Raven.

'I don't like it.' Juba came up beside her. 'If Father or Fronto were here they would forbid it.'

His moonlit face was becoming larger and his voice seemed unnaturally loud.

She knew the potion was beginning to take effect.

Suddenly, a small dark shape emerged from behind the woodpile, scampered across the clearing and leapt up on to Ursula.

'Meer!' She laughed as her big kitten clambered up her woollen cloak and crouched purring on her left shoulder.

Almost a year had passed since they had fled Rome one warm August night. Although Meer was almost as big as a full-grown cat, she still liked to perch on her mistress's shoulder.

Ursula's soul was loosening and she was about to send it into a mouse. This was not a good time for her big kitten to be here. She shifted the jar with the mouse to her left arm and tried to push Meer off.

But the big kitten stuck like a barnacle to a ship's bottom.

Finally, someone lifted Meer from her shoulder.

'Go quickly!' Bircha's voice seemed to come from a great

15

distance. 'I'll hold Meer. One of you take her to Snakebeard's Den!'

'I will.' Ursula was aware of Prasutus's hand on her waist, guiding her into a dim warm space. For a moment she was disappointed that it was not Raven. Or Castor. Then she remembered that Raven had left a month ago, and his twin Castor had gone to find him not long after.

Prasutus put a dimly burning oil-lamp on the floor of the small cave carved into the hillside. Then he helped Ursula sit cross-legged with her back against the earth wall of the den. When he had backed out and slid the plank barrier in front of the cave mouth, she scooped the mouse from his jar and put him down before her on the packed earth floor. The golden glow of the oil-lamp showed her his little nose twitching as he explored the new space.

She stared at the mouse, focusing all her attention on him. He stopped sniffing and stared back at her with jet-black eyes.

Ursula felt her soul loosen and detach.

Then, with a dizzy plunge, she fell into his tiny black gaze.

She had become a mouse.

Chapter Five
SCIRPI

U rsula knew her brother had been right to call it powerful and dangerous witchcraft when her soul fell into the mouse.

The cramped den now seemed like a vast cavern. Her twitching nose had suddenly become exquisitely keen. She could smell olive oil burning in the lamp, sawdust, four different types of leaves, two types of mould, linen, wool and the faintly musky scent of a giant mammal. After a moment, she realised the last smell was made by a human: herself!

She could see her human body sitting cross-legged, eyes closed, tendrils of black hair falling over her smooth brown cheeks.

Unlike her sense of smell, her vision was not keener.

But it was different. All the colours were altered as if her new world was made of metal.

She saw silvery brightness in the open space, but old gold where the floor met the wall of the den. Some instinct told her the dark gold was good and the dazzling silver was bad.

Her feet were extraordinary, like having four huge hands with which she could feel and sense and climb. The earth hummed beneath her mouse palms.

Then a faint but wonderful smell reached her.

Cheese!

Somewhere not too far away was cheese.

The smell of it pierced all the other aromas and went right down to her inmost being, tugging and pulling her to her left.

A dribble of pee leaked out from beneath her tail. She had a tail! The urine was making a hot glowing path on the beaten earth floor where she had been a moment before. The colour was beyond violet; it was a shade her human eyes had never beheld before.

The tantalising scent of cheese lured her to a gate of wooden slats. Impossible to get through, and yet her body would not be denied the cheese on the other side. Somehow, miraculously, she found a slight dip in the earth and pushed her nose into an impossibly narrow gap. She felt the pressure on the top of her skull and the bottom of her jaw. She let her internal organs compress sideways and more pee squeezed out. Her tail felt as big as a tree. It felt every change in texture.

Then she was through and out into the silver night!

The hoot of an owl sent a thrill of terror through her. She could see the looming shape of a huge round building on the horizon. *The cheese was in there!* Between her and the building was a vast plain. But already she was crossing it, running as fast as she could: going from clump of grass to leaf and anything else that would shelter her.

Abruptly, she was face-to-face with another mouse. This mouse was a male defending his territory.

She could smell his aggression.

See him curl back his upper lip.

See him reveal sharp teeth.

See him prepare to attack.

18

Suddenly, a shadow snatched him away.

No. Not a shadow.

An owl!

Squealing in terror, Ursula the mouse raced across the clearing and into the big building.

The earthen floor was covered by rushes. Beneath her paws they were as big as logs and it was hard going until she reached a place where they were crushed flat by human feet. The gloriously tangy scent was calling her to a high wooden platform set on four square trunks.

A table! The cheese was on a table!

She craved that cheese as she had craved nothing else in her life. The inner flesh of her cheeks spurted saliva into her mouth at the thought of it. Her pink nose twitched as the scent pulled her forward. Even her whiskers tingled.

And suddenly she was climbing up the tree-trunk table leg and on to the platform tabletop and at last she was upon the cheese. She became teeth and tongue and gullet, and the inexpressibly delicious taste of cheese.

For a blissful few moments she fed on the cheese, until a stab of fear arrived along with the stench of cat pee.

She froze.

Behind her, she heard something padding towards her. The almost silent paws of a giant predator.

Slowly, Ursula turned away from the brick of cheese.

A crouching feline watched Ursula with terrible unrecognising blue-grey eyes. Her shoulder blades were up and her tail twitched.

Meer was no longer kitten-sized.

She was panther-sized.

No. She was elephant-sized!

There was no way to escape this supremely dangerous animal.

19

She was doomed.

She was about to be devoured by the kitten she had risked her life to save.

Unless . . .

She remembered what Raven and Prasutus had taught her: that the magic loosened the soul so you could send it into another animal. If the magic was still strong enough, perhaps she could transfer her soul into Meer before she was devoured.

But it had never been attempted before.

Not even Raven had tried leaving one creature for another.

But she had to try.

She had to.

She summoned all her resolve and, as her big kitten pounced, Ursula sent her soul leaping into Meer's eyes.

I must get in, was her last thought as a mouse.

Chapter Six
FELES

Juba was fast asleep and dreaming of his family in Rome when a scream brought him instantly awake. It was very dim in the roundhouse but Juba could tell by light filtering through a thinning section of the conical thatch roof that it was already getting light outside. These British summer nights were the shortest he had ever known.

Bircha screamed again. Even in the murky gloom he could see her long silver-blonde hair. She was standing by the curved inner wall of the roundhouse, near the table. She held the water jug in one hand and a clay beaker in the other, frozen in the act of pouring a drink of water.

'Meer's got a mouse!' she cried. 'And I think it's Ursula!'

Juba scrambled to his feet and squinted at the table.

He saw Meer crouched on one corner of the table, behind bowls and cups near the mortar and pestle. The cat had something in her paws.

Juba cursed silently. He had left a brick of cheese there, only partly wrapped in a piece of cabbage tied with twine. He should have hung it from one of the two roof beams that made an X above them, along with their other stores, but he had wanted a snack before bed.

21

'Let her go!' Bircha squealed, and threw her beaker at the big kitten.

The beaker missed Meer but struck the whitewashed daub wall of the roundhouse, splashing it with water and then bouncing on to the earthen floor.

Absorbed by her prey, Meer did not even look up.

Juba took a cautious a step forward. The cat was definitely toying with something, but what?

The dim light in the roundhouse suddenly grew brighter as someone pulled back the deerskin flap over the door and let in a flood of early morning light. Out of the corner of his left eye, Juba saw a flash of copper-red hair and knew it was Bouda.

Resourceful, quick-thinking Bouda. Always good in a crisis. He allowed himself a flash of gratitude before returning his attention to the thing between the cat's paws.

Now he could hear squeaking.

The flood of light from the doorway showed that Meer definitely had a mouse.

But was Ursula's soul really in the mouse?

How was such a thing even possible?

He relaxed a little. She had only been studying Druid ways for a month, and everyone knew it took at least twenty years to achieve full mastery.

The mouse squeaked and his muscles tensed again.

What if it was true? What if Ursula's soul *was* somehow caught in the mouse and she could never return to her body?

'*What ARE you doing!*' cried a voice from above, and Loquax flew down from one of his favourite perches in the conical thatched roof.

Startled, Meer let the mouse go.

But only for an instant.

With a pounce that sent a cup rolling, Meer was at the other end of the table, pinning the mouse by its tail.

Loquax fluttered on to Bircha's shoulder. '*Carpe diem!*' said the mynah bird.

Juba pointed. 'Loquax! Attack!'

Loquax tipped his black head and regarded Juba brightly. '*Ave, Domitian!*' he said, and flew out the bright door of the roundhouse.

Juba cursed softly, then took a deep breath. 'Bouda?' he asked. 'Will you go to the Druid Den and see if Ursula is still in a trance or awake? If she's awake and in her right mind, we don't have to worry.'

Out of the corner of his left eye he saw the fiery gleam of Bouda's hair as she nodded. As she went to follow his instructions, the deerskin flap fell back and the roundhouse grew a little dimmer.

A figure moving on his right attracted his attention. It was Prasutus. He wore only his loincloth and held a stick with a fishing net at the end. Juba gave him a silent nod of approval.

Slowly, and without taking his eyes from cat and mouse, Juba crouched down. With his left hand, he groped for the beaker on the floor, the one Bircha had thrown. When he had it, he transferred it to his right hand and rose slowly to his feet.

'Nobody move,' Juba said in a low voice, aware of the others watching him to see what he would do.

All movement ceased in the roundhouse. Only the tip of Meer's tail twitched as she pinned the squeaking mouse to the tabletop.

Juba gripped the cup in his right hand. It was one of the high-quality imported beakers he had bought in Lactodurum two weeks before. A shipment of cups from Roman Gaul. Made

23

of shiny orange-red clay with vine leaves in slight relief curling on the surface, the cups had been more expensive than the local pottery. But they reminded him of home and so he had bought them.

The light in the roundhouse grew brighter again and Bouda's voice came softly from the door. 'Ursula's still in a trance, Juba. And there's no sign of the mouse that was with her. I think Bircha is right. I think Ursula is in that mouse.'

Juba's throat was suddenly dry.

He had not come all the way from Rome to Britannia to lose his sister to magic.

'Dear Mercury,' he prayed. 'If I get my sister back I vow I will get her out of this place.'

He pulled back his right arm.

On the table, the cat had stopped toying with the mouse. Juba knew it was now or never. Ursula would never forgive him if he killed her pet, but if he could just stun Meer and make her release the Ursula-mouse, then he might bring his sister back to this world.

He took careful aim and threw the cup at the same moment that Prasutus brought down the fishing net. But both of them were too slow for Meer, who was already down on the ground and trotting triumphantly for the open door, tail high and whiskers bright.

And with a mouse dangling from her jaws.

Chapter Seven
AVIS

Ursula had transferred from mouse to Meer just in time.

As a mouse, her craving for cheese had been compelling. Now that she was in a cat, her craving for mouse was irresistible.

The desire to devour something warm and chewy and crunchy and sweet overwhelmed her.

Every hair on her body was smooth with pleasure. Every double beat of her heart sent joy through her legs. The pads of her paws tingled. The tips of her whiskers sang. This was what she was made to do!

Far at the back of her head, the glimmer that was Ursula the Roman girl was horrified.

But that tiny human voice was dominated by the all-consuming bliss of her feline dilemma. She longed to crunch her prey but she also wanted to make the game last.

The mouse was quivering and alive on the sensitive pads of her paws as she batted it back and forth. Every time the mouse moved, it sent a tantalising savour up her nose. The skitter of its paws thrilled her ears. When she unsheathed the claws of her dominant forepaw and pricked it, the mouse's squeal sent a red jolt of pleasure shuddering through her, from the tip of her nose to the end of her tail.

Somewhere on the edge of her consciousness came a flutter of wings and for a moment instinct made her look up. It was the Bird again.

Distracted for a moment, her prey made a bolt for freedom. But she pounced and pinned it down.

She had it again, but now her pleasure was joined by a new desire: to get it safely away where she could devour it at leisure.

Sinking her teeth quickly into the mouse's neck, she trotted across the clearing. The sun was rising and the weight of the still-squirming mouse a pleasure promised. She hurried to the giant oak and went up its rough and fissured bark as easily as climbing a hill. When she reached her favourite perch, a branch from which she could see the clearing below, she settled down to eat the mouse.

The first few bites were joyous, for it was still warm and twitching. She relished the slight pressure on her teeth before they broke through the skin to the softer parts inside. She savoured the salty sweetness on her tongue along with the fullness of it in her gullet. Finally, she purred with satisfaction as it went right down to the core of her being.

Presently, the eating of the mouse became less of a pleasure, for it was cooling and one of its inner organs tasted bitter. She was growing bored.

Once again the flutter of wings and the strange croak of the black bird with the yellow beak made her look up. She loved hunting birds as much as she loved hunting furry things, but something deep within her knew that this bird was not like the others. This bird was inviolate. She was not allowed to harm him.

The Bird cocked his black head and regarded her with a bright eye.

Watching from the back of Meer's consciousness, Ursula realised this might be a way to exit the bloodthirsty kitten and achieve her heart's desire.

She gathered every particle of resolve and made her spirit leap into Loquax's eyes.

For a moment she was nowhere, floating in a fog that was not even white.

And the next she was flying.

Flying!

This was ten times better than being in her cat. A hundred times better than being in a mouse. The mouse's desire for food and the cat's urge to hunt were both tyrants. Those instincts demanded obedience. But flying was freedom, a joy in itself.

Her body felt light and strong and hollow.

Around her were the trees she had come to know so well in the past days. She had only to focus on one and she was moving towards it. Her wings, feathers and feet all knew what to do.

Somehow she knew which trees had the best grubs, the best perching twigs and the best viewpoints.

Stiffening her wings, she made a small leaning motion with her body so that the trees tilted and the ground fell away. She zoomed down to skim the sun-dappled ground, then soared up above the canopy of treetops.

Colours were different, too. She could see colours beyond red, before blue. Everything was sharply detailed. She could see every vein on every leaf, every bug on every twig, every pebble on the ground. Edible things were shades beyond red and harmful things the shades beyond blue. But she had gorged on berries earlier and was not hungry.

She went higher, and the trees shrank below her. Now she

could see a ribbon of road leading to a Man Nest: the place where People lived together. It was morning and the road was busy with Moving Boxes pulled by Four-Legs. There were People riding and also some Shiny People marching in rank, which always attracted her attention because they made a symmetrical pattern.

She flew down to have a closer look at the Shiny People.

Soldiers, said Ursula's consciousness at the back of her memory. That was the word: soldiers. There were lots of them. Like a silver caterpillar, their legs all moving together. For a while she flew above them, but presently felt an unease that told her she was straying too far from her base.

She wheeled back and saw two Glittery People riding Four-Legs. Their bodies sparkled like the scales of a fish.

The Fish-Scale People were talking and had stopped. One of them looked up and pointed at her. The second looked, too, and now they were taking out two sticks with bird feathers on one end and putting them in another curved stick with a string and pointing them at her.

Ursula tried to remember the word for this stick with feathers.

Arrow!

As if her naming it had released it, the arrow sped towards her and she saw its metal point coming towards her fast.

'*Carpe diem!*' she heard herself cry.

The arrow missed her by a bare wing's-breadth, and a moment later something fluttered past her.

Ursula watched a falcon plunge to the ground, an arrow in his chest.

The Fish-Scale People hadn't been trying to kill her. They had been trying to save her.

Flying closer, she saw one looked familiar, his skin colour a little darker than most.

Ursula was so excited that she flew back to the sacred grove to share her news.

Chapter Eight
VENEFICIUM

It was mid-morning.

Juba and the others had been sitting outside the Druid's Den, waiting for Ursula to come out of her trance, when he heard her moving inside.

'Ursula!' Juba leaned forward to peer into her cubbyhole. 'Are you all right?'

She nodded and whispered, 'Fronto's coming!'

'What are you talking about? He's been with the army since last year and is serving with the governor's bodyguard in Londinium.'

'I know,' she said. Even in the dim light he could see the pupils of her eyes were as big and black as olives. 'But I saw him. He's coming here.'

Juba made the sign against evil.

'I'm thirsty,' Ursula croaked. 'And hungry.'

'Here's some water,' said Bircha, pushing her arm past Juba's crouching body into the small underground den.

Ursula took the beaker and drank greedily, water running from the corners of her mouth, as if she had forgotten how to use a cup overnight.

'Food?'

'Not until the potion is out of her body,' came Prasutus's voice in Juba's ear. 'You'll know when her eyes look normal again. She drank far too much,' he muttered.

'No food, yet, Ursula,' said Juba. 'It might make you sick.'

'But I ate a mouse!' She shuddered. 'I can still taste it.'

Juba shook his head. 'I think you just imagined that,' he said. 'But here's some water with vinegar.'

This time Ursula drank the posca without spilling it, and even in the dim light her eyes did not seem as black. 'I didn't *imagine* eating a mouse,' she told him. 'I went from the mouse into Meer just in time. But eating was almost as horrible as being eaten. So I jumped from Meer to Loquax. And I flew, Juba. I flew!'

The urgency in her voice told Juba that she really believed what she was saying. He glanced at Bouda, the only other sceptic in the Druid school. She rolled her eyes and gave her head a tiny shake.

'So what did you see when you flew?' Bolianus leaned forward and spoke into the den.

'Did you see Raven?' asked silver-blonde Bircha over his shoulder.

'Come outside and tell us!' said Prasutus.

Ursula put up her left hand, like someone warding off evil. 'It's too bright out there,' she said. 'The light hurts my eyes.'

'Then come into the roundhouse,' said Juba. 'You've been sitting in this den since midnight and now it's morning.'

'All right. I'll close my eyes. You guide me.'

She shut her eyes and Juba helped her out. As he took her hand, he felt the bones. They had all lost weight this past month, despite his regular food runs to Lactodurum, but Ursula was the thinnest. This was partly due to their vegetarian diet, he thought with a sigh. And maybe also a result of her obsession with trees and animals.

The glade was dappled with shade but it was still bright enough to show him how grubby her face was. Lit by the greenish yellow glow of sun filtered by leaves, his sister looked jaundiced. She kept her eyes shut until they were back in the roundhouse.

Once inside, Juba guided his sister to the dimmest part of the bed shelf.

When the door flap was closed, Ursula opened her strange black eyes and told them about her adventures as mouse, cat and bird.

'I can't believe you advanced two levels in one night,' said Bircha, brushing back her pale blonde hair.

'Even Raven never jumped a level in one go,' said Bolianus.

Prasutus nodded. 'My grandfather told me it took him a year for each level.'

Their faces were full of something like awe as they looked at her. This annoyed Juba. The straight line of Bouda's mouth told him she felt the same.

'I think it was just a dream, Ursula,' Juba said. 'But that potion is very dangerous. I forbid you to practise magic or sorcery any more. Mater and Pater put me in charge of the family. They made me paterfamilias . . .'

'No.' Ursula calmly stroked Meer. 'It wasn't a dream. I really saw it. When I flew away from here, I saw the road from Lactodurum and a whole cohort of soldiers. I saw wagons going to market. And then I saw Fronto and his friend Vindex.'

'Impossible,' said Juba. 'They're at the fort in Londinium, miles from here.'

'I'm telling you: I saw them! And they fired an arrow at me

32

but they weren't shooting at me. They were shooting at a falcon that was about to kill me!'

'Fronto hit a falcon with an arrow?' Bolianus frowned. 'That's almost impossible to do. Maybe you dreamed that bit.'

'Then how did she know,' said a voice, 'that we were coming and that I made the shot of my life when I saved her bird?'

They all turned to the doorway of the small roundhouse.

The voice belonged to a brown-skinned youth in fish-scale armour. He had a smile on his face and a dead falcon in his hand.

Juba's jaw dropped.

It was his brother Fronto.

Chapter Nine
BENEFICIARII

Fronto hesitated at the doorway of the small roundhouse. His smile faded as he peered into its dim interior. It smelled strongly of woodsmoke and faintly of mould. He wondered if the rush mats covering the floor had begun to rot in the damp summer heat. At the fort in Londinium, where he was now stationed, the barracks slave boy changed the mats on the floor of the anteroom every other month.

Fronto tapped the doorframe: *right, left, right* and stepped into the roundhouse with his right foot first.

'You all remember Vindex, don't you?' He held back the deerskin door flap with his left hand. Vindex came in almost shyly, even though he was of the Belgae and had grown up in a roundhouse like this one.

The boys and girls came forward from where they had been sitting around Ursula. They all looked thinner than Fronto remembered. He noticed that all but Juba were barefoot.

The beautiful girl called Bircha came forward first. Her silver-blonde hair flowed from a centre parting with two narrow plaits at the front pulled back. The side plaits had a blue ribbon woven in and it perfectly matched the blue of her eyes. Fronto remembered how she had blown him a kiss at the amphitheatre in Isca a month before, and his face grew warmer.

Bouda was there, too: the flame-haired beggar-girl who had fascinated him from the first moment she had grabbed his hand and told him she needed his help. Her slanting green eyes always sent a strange thrill through him.

But before he could greet either of them, his sister Ursula pushed between them and threw her arms around him. A moment later she recoiled.

'Ow!' Ursula pouted and rubbed at the tender skin on the underside of her elbow. 'Your armour bit me!'

He laughed. 'You're not supposed to hug a soldier wearing lorica squamata.'

Then everybody was greeting everybody. In the swirl of greetings, Fronto was aware of Bouda kissing his left cheek and a few moments later Bircha kissed his right.

He shook his brother Juba's hand and looked around. 'Where are the other pupils?'

'Everybody except Prasutus went home to their villages,' said Bolianus. 'Including us. But our parents said we could come back here.'

Bircha smiled. 'They know we'll just run away again if they forbid us.'

Prasutus stepped forward. 'You killed a falcon with one arrow?' He took the dead bird almost reverently from Fronto's hand.

'*Carpe diem!*' Loquax fluttered down on to Ursula's shoulder and cocked his head at Fronto.

'That's his way of saying thank you!' said Ursula.

'You're welcome.' Fronto nodded at the talking bird. 'You saved our lives once in the necropolis outside Rome. How could I not help you?'

'You saved me, too, Fronto!' cried Ursula, jumping up and down and making Loquax flap off her shoulder. 'I drank an enchanted potion and became a mouse and then a cat and then I went into Loquax. I saw you on the road. I was in Loquax!'

Alarmed, Fronto made the sign against evil and turned to Juba. 'Are you letting her practise sorcery? That's very dangerous.'

Vindex nodded. 'It's like the part of the *Odyssey* where a witch turns men into pigs and other animals.' In response to Bircha's frown he said, 'It's a poem in ancient Greek. Fronto's been telling me the story.'

'You try saying no to Ursula,' said Juba.

'But look at her!' said Fronto. 'Her eyes look strange. Her face is scratched and her feet are filthy.' He looked at the others. 'And you've all lost weight. I don't think this place is good for you.'

'No, it's a wonderful place!' cried Ursula. 'We don't ever want to leave!'

Fronto squinted up at the conical roof. 'Your thatch needs repairing,' he said, then pushed some of the rushes on the floor with his toe. 'The floor needs changing; it smells like someone's been using it as a latrine.'

Juba cleared his throat and gestured at a pot of stew simmering over the central hearth fire. 'We're just about to eat,' he said. 'Will you join us?'

Fronto nodded. 'I'm ravenous!'

But Vindex narrowed his eyes at the cauldron. 'If we eat your stew, will it turn us into swine?'

Juba laughed and Ursula said, 'It's not a magic potion. It's just vegetable stew.'

Bircha was already ladling the stew into bowls. They sat cross-legged around the fire and after Prasutus asked the gods of the grove to bless the food, they ate.

After a few bites, Fronto looked up. 'No meat?'

Juba shook his head ruefully. 'No. We're a bit like the Pythagoreans here. No meat or beans allowed. Only vegetables and grain.'

Fronto looked at Ursula; his sister had refused to eat meat since the age of seven. 'No wonder you like it here.'

Ursula had been staring into the flames, transfixed. Now she looked up at him, her eyes glowing like emeralds in the firelight. 'Oh, Fronto,' she cried. 'I love it here. There are trees and animals and we don't eat meat and we're kind to each other. We only have to do a little weaving while we recite the sacred texts. And today I flew for the first time, and Raven will be so proud of me when he comes back. I never, ever want to leave!'

Fronto and Vindex looked at one another and then down at their bowls.

'What is it?' cried Ursula. 'Why are you looking at each other like that?'

Fronto took a deep breath. 'We've come to ask you to leave,' he said. 'We're going on a quest.'

Chapter Ten
LEGATIO

At the thought of leaving the Druid academy, Juba felt a wave of relief wash over him. *Thank you, Jupiter and Mercury,* he said to himself. He turned to Fronto. 'You're going on a quest? And you want us to come with you?'

'The other way round,' said Fronto. 'You're being sent on a quest and Vindex and I are coming along to protect you.'

He removed his conical helmet with its white ostrich feather, and also the felt skullcap he wore underneath. Although his hair was strangely short, he looked like Fronto again. 'Our patroness Flavia Gemina has a mission for us.' He ran a hand through his dark curls.

'Flavia Gemina?' said Prasutus. 'Who's she?'

'She befriended us when we first arrived in this province,' said Fronto. 'She offered us protection. In return we go on secret quests for her from time to time. Like us, she hates the Emperor Domitian.'

Juba felt a jolt of alarm at the mention of the hated name. 'Shhhh!' he hissed, looking around.

Bouda rolled her eyes. 'Who's going to hear us, Juba? We're in a secret grove miles from the nearest town.'

Juba flushed. 'You can't be too careful,' he said. 'They throw people to the beasts for such talk.'

Fronto continued with lowered voice. 'Flavia Gemina lives in the governor's palace in Londinium. Her husband is one of the governor's close friends and advisors.' He looked around at them. 'You know that Vindex and I are now part of the governor's special troops?'

'Of course we do,' said Bouda. 'We were there when he invited you to join his bodyguard.'

Juba turned to Fronto. 'You said Flavia Gemina had a new quest for us. Who does she want us to find?'

'His name is Jonathan ben Mordecai.'

Bouda frowned. 'Strange name.'

'Yes,' said Fronto. 'And he might be calling himself something else.'

'Not much to go on,' said Juba. 'How old is he? Was he kidnapped? Or did he run away?'

'He's not a child,' said Fronto. 'He's a doctor. An old friend of Flavia Gemina's.' Fronto pulled his wax tablet from his belt and flipped it open. '*Square face, dark curly hair, husky and slightly melancholic.*'

Ursula scowled. 'I don't want to quest for a doctor; I want to stay here. Raven could return any day. Anyway, I thought we were supposed to be looking for children or young people, not adults.'

Juba shrugged. 'Flavia Gemina appointed us as questors. We can search for anything we like.'

'Anything *she* likes,' muttered Ursula.

Juba frowned. 'Why does Flavia Gemina want us to find her old friend?'

Fronto lowered his voice even more. 'Apparently, he has information that could bring down the Emperor Domitian.' He took a breath and continued. 'With Domitian out of the way,' he said, 'we could all return to Italy. Not just us, but also Flavia Gemina, along with her friends and family.'

Hope sparked in Juba's heart. Then a question arose in his mind. 'So why doesn't Doctor Jonathan bring this information directly to Flavia Gemina?'

'He doesn't know she's here in Britannia.'

'Where would we even start to look for a doctor who might be living under another name?' asked Bouda.

Fronto consulted his wax tablet. 'To find Doctor Jonathan, we need the help of another one of Flavia Gemina's childhood friends. His name is Lupus and he became a famous dancer.'

Bircha had gone to get a platter of hazelnut and honey cakes. She was extending them to Fronto, but when he said this she froze. She and her brother looked at each other with wide eyes.

'Not *the* Lupus? The famous pantomime dancer?' Bolianus cried.

'You've heard of him?' asked Fronto, stretching to get a cake.

Brother and sister nodded.

'We saw him half a year ago in Calleva Atrebatum,' said Bolianus.

'He was amazing!' gushed Bircha. 'And so were his musicians. Watching them made me want to join a pantomime troupe. I practised my flute for months afterwards and thought of running away to join them.'

'It's true,' said Bolianus. 'She did. And I thumped a drum to keep her company.'

Juba drained his cup and set it down. 'So Flavia Gemina wants us to find this pantomime dancer so he can help us find Jonathan?'

'*Find Jonathan!*' said Loquax from Ursula's shoulder.

Fronto's mouth was full of honey cake, so he nodded.

Vindex said, 'We don't know what Jonathan looks like but Lupus does; that's why we need his help. Lupus is going to meet us in a town called Viroconium, about eighty miles north of here, on the Nones of July. Then we'll all join up with a troupe of gladiators touring the forts and fortresses of Britannia.'

Juba's thoughts were in turmoil. A few moments before, he had been longing to leave the grove, but this particular quest set off alarm gongs in his head.

He looked at Fronto. 'If we become part of a travelling show going to forts and fortresses, then people might recognise us.'

'Don't worry,' said Fronto. 'You'll only be helping behind the scenes.' He took a wax tablet from his belt. 'I have a document from the governor promising protection and free passage to an unnamed number of helpers who will assist Lupus the Pantomime Dancer at a series of games in honour of Domitian.'

'*Ave Domitian!*' said Loquax.

The mention of their mortal enemy Domitian made Juba shudder. The evil emperor had issued a warrant for their arrest and a reward for their capture.

'And if we don't want to go on this quest?' he ventured.

Fronto and Vindex exchanged a glance. 'I'm afraid you have no choice,' Fronto told them. 'You have to come with us. All of you.'

Chapter Eleven
RECUSATIO

When Fronto announced that they had to leave Mistletoe Oak, Ursula felt hot anger bubble up in her chest.

'I refuse to go!' She stamped her foot. 'We love it here. We're waiting for Raven to come back and teach us more about Druidic ways, aren't we?'

Bolianus, Bircha and Prasutus nodded enthusiastically, but Juba and Bouda avoided her gaze.

Fronto sighed. 'Would it help if I told you that Jonathan came to Britannia to look for his kidnapped nephew?'

Ursula looked at him, puzzled.

'Remember when we first met Flavia Gemina, she told us about all her adventures with her three close friends? Jonathan was one of them. When he was thirteen, his sister Miriam gave birth to identical twins. She named them Soter and Philadelphus. Soso and Popo for short. When they were only a few months old, Popo was kidnapped.'

'Raven!' Ursula's heart skipped a beat. 'Popo grew up to be Raven! And Soso is Castor!'

'Doctor Jonathan is the twins' uncle?' said Juba.

Fronto nodded. 'He's been searching for Raven since he was about thirteen. He's been to almost every province in the Roman

Empire. And now he's here in Britannia. He's vowed not to stop his quest until he finds Raven.'

Ursula frowned. 'Why does Flavia Gemina want us to find Jonathan? Can't the pantomime dancer find him?'

'Because if we can tell the doctor that Raven is alive and well, he'll finally be free to turn his attention to bringing down our mutual enemy,' said Fronto. 'She thinks we have a better chance of finding Jonathan and convincing him to use his information if we pool our resources.'

Ursula glanced at her three young Druid friends, then back at Fronto. 'Why don't we wait here for Raven? He went to see his mother, but he loves this grove and these three are his friends. If he comes here, then the doctor might follow, which means we would be the first to find Jonathan!'

'*Find Jonathan!*' echoed Loquax from Ursula's shoulder.

'Good idea,' said Prasutus. He turned to Fronto. 'Why don't you take Juba and Bouda on your quest but leave Ursula here with us? We can carry on our studies and if Raven or Doctor Jonathan show up we'll keep them here.'

Fronto shook his head. 'I'm afraid you can't remain here.' His fish-scale armour glittered as he turned to look at Bircha and Bolianus. 'Nor can you,' he said. 'You can either return to your families or come with us.'

'Why?' Bircha's blue eyes were wide.

'Because some of the governor's other advisors found out about this place,' said Fronto. 'And now that they know, he has ordered it to be destroyed. To show mercy would be seen as a sign of weakness. Romans hate and fear Druids more than any one else.'

'No!' cried Ursula. Meer jumped off her as she stood up, and Loquax fluttered around her head as she ran out of the roundhouse and across the dappled clearing to the ancient oak.

When she reached it, the deep fissures of the trunk helped her climb. She used toes as well as fingers and was soon in one of the higher branches.

'Grandfather Oak!' she whispered, putting her arms around the branch and pressing her ear to it. 'I don't want to leave you or this place. I love the trees and animals. And Raven might come back any day! Tell me what to do!' The bark was even rougher than Fronto's bronze scale armour, but she endured the discomfort to hear the tree's advice.

At first she only heard the soft rustle of the breeze in the leaves, the tinkling wind chimes in the lower branches and a few sleepy bird cheeps. She took a deep breath and held it, along with her thoughts.

Then she heard it: a voice like distant thunder, a soft whisper around a core of huge power.

'*Farewell.*' The Oak's voice held infinite sadness.

A moment later, Loquax landed on a branch above her. '*Find Jonathan!*' he urged.

With a sob of anguish, Ursula lowered herself from the lowest branch. When her feet were on solid ground again, she turned and saw the others. The seven of them were standing in the glade looking at her.

Bathed in the gold-green light of early afternoon, they appeared as strange but beautiful creatures.

Vindex and her brother Fronto were glittering fish-men.

Willowy Bircha, her pale blonde hair almost green in the light of the glade, was a slender sapling.

Bolianus resembled his Druid name, Hawk, given to him on account of his feathery hair, strong nose and keen eyes.

With her slanting green eyes and coppery hair, Bouda was a beautiful fox.

44

Prasutus was a cooling ember, the same colour as his hair.

And Juba's brown skin, tawny cloak and worried eyes reminded her of a faithful watchdog.

Looking at them, Ursula felt a sudden overwhelming surge of love. It poured out of her and crashed against them like a wave.

But when it rolled back and swallowed her, everything went white.

Chapter Twelve
CONVULSIO

Juba was horrified to see Ursula's eyes roll back into her head.
She slumped back against the oak tree and he only just
managed to run forward and catch her before she struck the
earth. Her body was both stiff and trembling as he eased her to
the ground.

Meer emerged from some bushes and Loquax flew about
their heads crying, '*Ave Domitian! Carpe diem! Find Jonathan!*'

'What's happening?' Fronto clanked as he jogged over to
them. When he saw Ursula's white eyes and foaming mouth,
he made the sign against evil. So did Vindex, but Bouda knelt
down and gently held Ursula's shoulders.

'Something's wrong.' Bouda looked up at Juba. 'I don't think
this is a faint. She's trembling'

'It's a seizure!' cried Bircha, wringing her hands together.

'An evil spirit!' Fronto took a step back. 'She's possessed by
an evil spirit!'

'No,' said Juba. 'It must be caused by the potion she drank.'

Prasutus was on his knees beside her. 'I think you're right.'
His face was full of concern. 'I should never have let her drink
all that potion last night; it was too much.'

Ursula's stiff body was shivering violently.

Bolianus also knelt beside Ursula. 'Get me a leather strap!' he cried. 'Or a twig! Our aunt used to have seizures. If you don't put a wood or leather between the person's jaws they can break their teeth or bite their tongue.'

'Look!' Bircha screamed and pointed. Blood was mixed with the foam coming out of the corners of Ursula's mouth.

'Too late,' said Prasutus grimly. 'Her jaw is locked anyway.'

Juba felt a chill run over him. He also made the sign against evil, but knew it was a feeble gesture. He knelt beside Bouda, who was wiping the bloody foam from Ursula's cheeks with her sleeve.

'Mercury,' he whispered, clutching the little statue of the god that he always carried down the front of his tunic. 'Please help her!'

Ursula was still shaking, her body rigid as a plank, and he fought back tears of frustration.

Then someone took his free hand. It was Bouda. She looked at him and he saw her eyes were also swimming. She squeezed his hand and he squeezed back. Then they turned their attention back to Ursula.

Her fit lasted for no more than fifty heartbeats, but it seemed an eternity to Juba.

When it was finally over, his sister's body relaxed and her breathing became slow and steady.

'She just needs to sleep,' said Bolianus. 'Then she should be fine.'

They wrapped her in blankets, took her into the roundhouse and placed her on the bed shelf.

Juba sat beside her. 'As soon as Ursula is recovered,' he said to the others, 'I'm taking her away from this place. We'll go on the quest.' He glanced at Bouda. 'Will you come with us?'

She gave a small nod.

Hawk-nosed Bolianus and his silver-blonde sister Bircha looked at each other. 'Can we come with you, too?' Bolianus asked Juba. 'We have nowhere else to go.'

Juba looked at Fronto. 'If it's all right with my brother.'

Fronto nodded. 'The tablet says helpers. It doesn't specify how many. Or what their jobs will be.'

'May I come, too?' asked Prasutus, with a quick glance at Ursula.

'Yes, but no magic,' said Juba. 'And no mention of Druids, especially after last month's near rebellion. The Romans will throw us to the beasts if they think we have anything to do with Druidism.'

'I promise,' said Prasutus.

Fronto nodded and made some notes in his wax tablet.

Juba noticed that Ursula was awake and struggling to sit upright in her bed of furs.

'Are you all right, Ursula?' He helped her sit. She nodded and tried to speak, but her bitten tongue would not let her make words. Finally, she pointed at Fronto's wax tablet and mimed writing. Bouda reached into the front of her tunic and pulled out the wax tablet she used for her lessons with Juba.

Ursula took the bronze stylus in a trembling hand and wrote on it.

Juba read it out: PLEASE DON'T LET THE ROMANS BURN THIS GROVE.

Prasutus knelt beside the bed shelf and took Ursula's hand.

'The best way of protecting the grove,' he said, 'is to go away and leave no trace that we were ever here.'

Ursula blinked a few times, then nodded.

Juba went to the doorway of the roundhouse and looked around the grove.

'Let's spend the rest of the day removing all traces of Druidism. Then we can go.'

Chapter Thirteen
CARRUCA

All the tears Ursula had never cried growing up in Rome, she shed the day they left the grove called Mistletoe Oak.

Juba and Fronto had taken down the tents and packed them in a big white ox-drawn carriage. This carruca had been given to them by their uncle nine months before.

Prasutus and Bolianus had filled in the den carved into the hillside, while Bircha had planted some stinging nettles to cover the scar.

As the best climber in the group, Ursula herself took down every votive tied to the branches of the ancient oak. Each ribbon, strand of wool or scrap of tin represented a prayer or vow of thanks, and as she pulled them off she asked Grandfather Oak to grant the prayers. Finally, she took down the tintinnabula with its tiny bronze bells.

Vindex had used a fallen branch to rake the floor rushes out of the roundhouse and into the clearing. In place of the rushes, he had strewn the floor of the roundhouse with hay and manure from the stables tent. This would cover traces of a hearth fire and make it look as if only animals had dwelt there. They couldn't completely hide the fact that people had been living here, but they could make it look like something other than a Druid retreat.

Into the storage area beneath the benches of the ox-drawn carruca went their sleeping skins, rugs, cups, beakers and spoons along with the dismantled loom and its half-finished bolt of nettle-cloth. There was also a thick sheaf of nettle stems, retted and dried and ready for pounding. Also, a big basket of pale gold nettle fluff, already carded and ready for spinning. Bouda had discovered a love for weaving; she claimed it calmed her and helped her achieve *ataraxia*, a sense of stoical calm.

They packed their two long-handled fishing nets, an axe for chopping wood and three iron-tipped hunting javelins, grown rusty with disuse. Most of their clothes were those they wore on their backs, but they also found four white hooded cloaks woven of the finest wool.

Everyone knew that Druids wore white, but the robes were far too valuable to be burned. It was Bircha's idea to make dye in the small bronze cauldron that they used for stew and potion. Bouda and Bircha boiled some ivy leaf with copper scrapings and dyed one cloak pale green. Using onionskin and copper, they dyed another cloak fox-red. Onionskin with iron mordant turned the third cloak nut-brown and they bathed the final cloak in hot water and elderberries until it came out pale lavender. Bouda and Bircha spread the cloaks over shrubs and bushes in the sunniest part of the grove to let them dry.

Finally, there was a beautiful ceremonial cape of black and pine green cormorant feathers. It reminded Ursula of the first time she had heard the trees speak and of her brief but memorable flight as Loquax, and she could not bear to destroy it. However, as it might betray their Druidic association, she packed it carefully at the very bottom of the storage area beneath the carruca benches.

51

Everything else they burned on the pile of sour rushes as the long summer evening grew dusky.

Twenty-four hours earlier, Ursula had been cutting mistletoe from the highest branches of the oak. Now she was watching smoke and sparks float up, a funeral pyre of a life that she had loved: an all-too-brief sojurn among trees, animals and birds.

That night they slept outside under the stars, rolled up fully dressed in their cloaks and sleeping skins. Ursula's bitten tongue throbbed and she wept more hot tears, until the consoling warble of a nightingale lulled her to sleep.

The next morning, they left at dawn in two small chariots and the big carruca with the two young soldiers riding ahead.

Ursula's tongue was even more swollen than the previous day and she felt drained. She did not even have enough strength to take the reins of the gentle white oxen whom she had once named Potens and Volens.

So she sat between Bouda and Juba with Meer on her left shoulder and Loquax fluttering up ahead, and she let the last of her tears fall.

Finally, the rocking motion of the cart and the dull rumble of wheels on the road sent her into a feverish sleep.

By the time they rumbled over a wooden bridge at midday, Ursula's skin was as hot as flatbread not turned over, so they moved her into the carruca and she stretched out on one of the padded benches. Bouda went in with her to sponge her forehead and give her sips of water whenever she woke.

When Ursula's fever finally broke and she struggled back to the surface of consciousness, she sensed that days had passed since they left Mistletoe Oak.

The carruca was silent and unmoving, but she could hear music and laughter from somewhere outside.

Ursula sat up, dizzy in the hot, dim interior. A beam of bright sunlight was shining through one of the small windows and a faint breeze brought a familiar scent along with the sound of flute, lyre and tambourine.

Puzzled, Ursula stood and went to the carriage door. Pushing it open, she was amazed to see a hot blue sky, a yellow sun and a green vineyard.

Could it be that she was back in Italy?

2

Chapter Fourteen
PANTOMIMUS

Ursula came carefully down the steps at the back of the carruca and shaded her eyes against brilliant light. The afternoon sun was hot on her arms and the poplar-lined road dissolved in a blur of heat haze in the distance. On both sides were vineyards: rows of young elm trees with grape vines coiling up around their trunks. It looked just like the countryside of Naples where her family had once owned a summer retreat.

Had she become a bird again and flown home?

No. The familiar smell of the oxen told her she was still in Britannia.

The sound of music and laughter was louder now that she was outside, and it brought her round to the side of the wagon. For a moment she stood still as a statue, frozen by the sight of two huge blue eyes painted on the back of a carruca parked further up the road. Because the carruca had a curved top, it looked like a giant face, with the eyes staring back at her above the heads of her friends.

Ursula's swollen tongue made it too painful to talk, so she came quietly up behind them.

She could not see the musicians yet, only the dazzling bronze fish-scale of Fronto and Vindex's armour. The two empty chariots were pulled up by the side of the road and the four ponies stood with their heads down, grazing.

'*Salve, Ursula!*' cried Loquax, flying down from his perch on the snow-white carruca and landing on her shoulder. '*Carpe diem!*'

On the road ahead, Juba turned, and his smile became broader when he saw her. 'Ursula!' he cried. 'You're awake! Are you feeling better?' Without waiting for her reply he said, 'Come look at this!'

Prasutus ran to her and gave her his arm, for she was still unsteady on her feet. Ursula moved forward beside him, eager to see what her brothers and friends were laughing at.

The answer was three musicians and a dancing dog.

Ursula looked at the dog first. She was small and white, with a conical cap of saffron-yellow felt and a collar that jingled as she stood on her hind legs and turned in place. Behind her stood three musicians in colourful tunics. A man in sea-foam green played a flute, a young woman in apricot played a kind of harp, and a man in dusty pink played a tambourine.

Glaring protectively over all of them were the two huge eyes painted on the back of the carruca. Set between the eyes, the pink painted door looked like a nose.

'Ursula!' Silver-blonde Bircha came hurrying over and gripped her arm, causing Loquax to flutter. 'He's here! He's in there!' She pointed at the carruca.

Ursula frowned and shook her head, as if to say, *Who?*

'Look!' Fronto also pointed at the carruca.

Ursula knew that eyes painted on something turned away evil. She let go of Prasutus's arm and, to show them she understood, she nodded and pointed at her own eyes, then made the sign against evil by pushing the palm of her left hand forward.

'No! Not the eyes. The writing,' said Fronto. 'See the letters?'

That was when Ursula saw that the black eyebrows above the eyes were actually letters. *LVPVS PANTOMIMVS*, they said: LUPUS the PANTOMIME.

Ursula had no idea why this was exciting. Once again she shook her head.

'Lupus the Pantomime Dancer!' said Bolianus.

'The one we were telling you about!' Bircha added.

'One of Flavia Gemina's childhood friends,' said Juba. 'The one who's going to help us on our quest to find the doctor with information that can defeat our enemy.'

'We think he's in there!' added Vindex, almost as excited as Bircha.

'Apparently he's world-famous,' said Prasutus with a grin.

The musicians were still playing their jaunty song and the little dog was still dancing on her hind legs, when Meer emerged from behind a poplar at the side of the road.

Seeing the cat, the little dog suddenly went back down on to four paws. The musicians let their song trail off comically, like a pig's bladder ball deflating.

'*Meeer!*' Ursula's cat meowed as she stalked towards the small white dog in its saffron-yellow cap.

'*Carpe diem!*' observed Loquax from Ursula's right shoulder.

Ursula offered a quick but fervent prayer to Venus that Meer would behave herself.

When the little dog and the big kitten stood nose to nose, Ursula could see that they were about the same size.

The dog's collar jingled as she wagged her tail.

Meer hissed and made her fur big.

Everyone laughed as the little dog retreated under the carruca, while the three musicians played running music, the theme of the fugitive slave from musical comedies.

Meer let her fur go smooth again, then turned and sauntered back towards Ursula, her tail erect.

The three musicians now played the theme of the pompous general from comic theatre.

Meer ignored their laughter and ascended to Ursula's left shoulder in a dignified manner.

But laughter and music both ceased as the back door of the pantomime wagon started to open. The musicians stood back. Now Ursula could see red-painted steps leading down from the door. This made the giant face at the back of the carriage seem to stick out its tongue. And now a young man appeared in the nose door. He had dark, shaggy hair and wore a short-sleeved sea-green tunic that showed skinny but muscular arms. He was stretching and yawning but suddenly froze, as if he had only just noticed his little audience.

Bircha laughed and clapped her hands and Vindex guffawed.

The man looked down in surprise as the small white dog jingled up the cherry-red steps and between his legs to safety. Then he looked back up at his audience, bug-eyed.

His eyes were lined with kohl, like a lady's, and they were echoed by the big eyes painted either side of him.

Everyone was laughing.

Everyone except for Ursula, who stood transfixed.

She knew she would never forget this moment: the moment she first saw Lupus, the world-famous pantomime dancer.

Chapter Fifteen
LINGUA

It was said of Lupus the Pantomime that he could speak more eloquently with his body and hands than most people could with their mouths.

So at first Ursula did not think it strange when he remained silent.

'You're him, aren't you?' Bircha looked up at him with awe. 'You're Lupus the famous pantomime dancer!'

The young man in the doorway nodded his shaggy head and gestured towards the words painted above him, bold in the morning sunshine:

LUPUS the PANTOMIME

'We saw you in Calleva Atrebatum last year,' said Bolianus. 'You were amazing.'

Lupus gave a little bow.

Fronto stepped forward, and as he moved, brilliant splinters of light bounced off his fish-scale armour. 'Greetings, Lupus Pantomimus,' he recited. 'We have been sent by your friend and our patroness Flavia Gemina to accompany you in your travels. She believes you can help us find a man by the name of Jonathan ben Mordecai, also known to you. He has information vital to the downfall of our mutual enemy—'

Lupus stopped him by thrusting both arms forward, palms out in the double sign against evil. Then he pressed his forefinger dramatically to his lips and swivelled his eyes from side to side, as if looking for spies.

Ursula knew Fronto would never name their enemy, but Lupus's rebuke had confused him. Fronto closed his mouth, then opened it, then closed it again.

Juba came to his brother's rescue. 'Are we permitted to tell you who we are?' he asked.

Lupus inclined his head in gracious assent.

'My name is Lucius Domitius Juba,' said Juba. 'My older brother Fronto just addressed you, and that's his comrade Vindex. They are both seconded from the First Cohort of Hamian Archers to the governor as scouts. May I also introduce Bouda and Prasutus of the Iceni, plus Bircha and her brother Bolianus of the Belgae?'

As he introduced them, each one said, 'Salve!' and Lupus bowed back.

Ursula tugged Juba's tunic.

Juba laughed. 'Oh! And my sister Ursula! Please excuse her,' he added, 'she bit her tongue a few days ago and can't talk.'

For a moment, Lupus stood as still as a statue. Then he jumped lightly down to the sunny road, his small orange cape fluttering behind him. Ignoring the others, he came straight towards Ursula.

She took an involuntary step backwards as he stopped before her. Close up, she could see the kohl-lined eyes beneath strong black brows were a bright sea-green, the same colour as his tunic. He turned his head to look at Loquax, perched on her shoulder.

'*Ave, Domitian!*' said her bird politely.

Lupus's eyes bugged out dramatically and he jumped back with both hands up.

Everybody laughed except Ursula.

Why hadn't he said anything? Was he mocking her inability to speak?

Lupus started to turn his head towards Meer, then quickly looked back at Loquax.

'*Ave, Domitian!*' Loquax said again, this time with less conviction.

The troupe of musicians had come up behind him. They were laughing, too.

Once again, Lupus started to turn his head to examine Meer, then turned back to stare accusingly at Loquax.

'*What ARE you doing?*' said Loquax.

This got the biggest laugh of all and even Lupus himself grinned. He then bowed to Ursula and reached up to stroke Meer, who purred contentedly.

Ursula was suddenly furious. Her swollen tongue was throbbing and he was making it a joke, just to get an easy laugh.

She took a step back and narrowed her eyes at him.

Lupus froze, mid-stroke. His smile faded and he looked genuinely surprised. Then he frowned and gave an inquisitive shake of his head, as if to ask how he had offended her.

He *still* refused to talk!

Ursula wanted to tell him she didn't care if he was world-famous. She wanted to shout that it was cruel to make fun of someone's disability. But she couldn't shout it. She couldn't even whisper it.

Then she remembered the wax tablet she had borrowed from Bouda. She fished down the front of her tunic and found it nestled above her belt.

Juba had addressed Lupus in Latin, so she used the same language to write: IT IS VERY CRUEL TO MOCK SOMEONE WHO CAN'T SPEAK!

The letters were wobbly with anger.

Then she held it up so he could see it.

When Lupus read it his green eyes grew wide. Then he shook his head and gave a sad smile. He undid a special pouch on his belt and took out a wax tablet of his own. It was the same size as hers but made of finely grained boxwood, and on the outside someone had painted a striking portrait of a dark-eyed young man. When Lupus opened it she caught a whiff of honey; it was made with the finest beeswax.

I CAN'T SPEAK EITHER, he wrote.

For a moment, silence ruled the bright road among the vineyards under the hot sun. It was so quiet that Ursula could hear skylarks high above and the crickets below.

Behind Lupus, someone stepped forward. It was the female lyre player, a slender young woman with bright eyes and dark hair.

'We thought everybody knew the story of how Lupus came to be a pantomime dancer,' she said softly. 'When he was only six years old, someone cut out his tongue.'

Chapter Sixteen
GREX

Later, in the lavender dusk of a summer evening on the outskirts of Viroconium, Ursula learned Lupus's sad story when he and his troupe put on a private show.

Because it was a warm, dry evening, they had made camp on a grassy verge near a brook and dined simply on local bread and cheese. Because of her sore tongue, Ursula had sipped buttermilk through a hollow river reed. She noticed that Lupus had carefully drunk a kind of soup prepared for him by the lyre-player. Her name was Clio and she was obviously devoted to him.

Ursula was still sipping her buttermilk as the musicians took up their instruments and stood in front of their carruca. Its side was painted with flat-topped parasol pines in the foreground and a double-peaked mountain in the distance. She recognised the Bay of Naples with blasted Vesuvius. The musicians began to play and Clio announced that they were going to perform *The Story of Lupus*.

Usually the pantomimus wore a mask, but this was Lupus's own story, so he used his own face, almost as eloquent as his body.

In a clear voice, Clio sang how, as a child, Lupus had

witnessed a murder and run away. But the killer caught him and cut out his tongue to prevent him from talking.

At this, Ursula put down her beaker of buttermilk, her appetite gone. Meer had been cleaning herself, but Ursula needed comfort so she picked up her cat. Meer's purring and the warmth of her furry body consoled Ursula a little.

Dancing on a patch of close-cropped grass with the scent of vineyards and the sound of crickets filling the twilight, Lupus showed how, at the age of only eight, three other children had found and befriended him. Clio sang how their kindness changed his life. She sang of the Roman girl named Flavia and her slave girl Nubia. She sang how the Jewish boy, Jonathan ben Mordecai, had invited Lupus to live and study with him, and how they became closer than brothers.

Ursula continued to stroke her cat as Clio sang of the terrible eruption of a volcano near Pompeii. Ursula knew about this because of their summer villa near Naples and because the volcano had exploded the year Fronto was born.

Clio sang of pirates who kidnapped children in the days that followed the volcano's eruption. She sang of sea voyages and shipwrecks, of gladiators and charioteers, of Egyptian crocodiles and Libyan caravans.

And all this time, Lupus supplemented her words with his movement, becoming crocodile and camel as well as emperor, eunuch and slave girl.

Then Lupus and his troupe performed the saddest story of all. It started happily with the birth of identical twins to Jonathan's sister Miriam. The baby boys were healthy and beautiful, sang Clio, with black hair and grey eyes. But soon the story grew sad on account of the death of the parents and later the kidnapping of one of the twins, Popo.

Ursula stopped petting Meer to wipe away tears. The thought of baby Raven being taken from his brother Castor made her heart ache more than her tongue.

Ursula glanced at Bouda, who was sitting next to her. Tears were running down the British girl's face. Ursula suspected that Bouda also loved the twins, but she didn't mind. She had decided that she would have Raven and Bouda could marry Castor. If only they could find them.

Looking around at the others, Ursula realised that everyone else was weeping. Everyone except her stoical brother Juba, whose jaw was clenched as he tried to control his emotions.

Clio sang of the death of the Emperor Titus and how his brother Domitian had banished Flavia, Nubia, Lupus and Jonathan from Italy after they tried to find the cause of Titus's death. It was while in exile that Jonathan resumed the search for his kidnapped nephew Popo. He had become a travelling doctor, treating everyone from babies to gladiators. For this part of the story, Lupus carried an imaginary walking stick and used his small orange cape to imitate a hooded cloak. He showed Jonathan shading his eyes against the sun in hot places, shivering by a fire in cold ones, standing under a tree or colonnade in wet countries.

Jonathan had been searching, sang Clio, for more than thirteen years.

For the first time, Ursula didn't mind that they were looking for Flavia Gemina's friend Jonathan.

She had been seeking Raven for only a few weeks. Castor had been trying to find his lost brother for over a year. But Doctor Jonathan had devoted half his life to this quest. Maybe Flavia Gemina was right: if they pooled their resources and brought

Doctor Jonathan face-to-face with Raven, he could finally rejoice in the knowledge that his nephew was safe.

Then they could move on with their most important task of all: defeating the tyrant who had sent them into exile.

Chapter Seventeen
RIVUS

The musicians had finished playing, and Lupus bowed. For a long moment there was silence. Then they all clapped, using curved hands like roof-tiles: the highest type of applause.

Ursula saw that Lupus was dripping with sweat. After taking a bow, he headed away from the camp in the direction of the brook.

Clio disappeared into the pantomime wagon while the other two musicians came to sit by the fire.

'May I see your flute?' Bircha asked the older musician. His name was Silenos because he looked like the snub-nosed, pot bellied god of the woods. He and the young drummer called Eros were both from Ephesus and spoke with Greek accents, when they spoke at all.

Silenos handed his flute to Bircha and she played one of the melodies from the pantomime. Bolianus borrowed the tambourine and beat the time. Everyone gasped in astonishment, and Bircha laughingly reminded them that she and her brother had practised the songs after hearing them the first time.

Clio came down the steps of the pantomime wagon, holding the little white dog.

'This is Issa,' she said, 'dearer to me than anyone. Except Lupus, of course.'

She fished a small red ball from her belt-pouch and tossed it into the dusky vineyard. Little Issa raced after it and when she brought it back they all took turns throwing it.

Ursula gazed at Clio in admiration. The singer was small and slender but Ursula could see she had a dancer's body. And her little dog Issa adored her.

'That was an amazing story,' said Bouda. 'Was it all true?'

Clio nodded. 'Every bit. Poor Lupus,' she added. 'He and Jonathan were such close friends. But he hasn't seen him for years. I think he misses him terribly.'

'Because he's been searching for Raven, the kidnapped twin,' muttered Juba. Ursula could hear the resentment in his voice.

'You've met Raven, haven't you?' Clio tossed the ball for Issa. 'Tell me about him.'

The others began telling Clio what they knew about Raven. How he had been raised by a Druid named Snakebeard who hated all Romans. How shocked he had been when he came face-to-face with Castor a few weeks before.

'He never even suspected he had a brother,' said Bolianus, 'much less an identical twin of Roman birth.'

Prasutus took over to tell Clio how the twins had argued and how Raven had attacked his brother.

He told how Raven had galloped off to find his mother and hear the truth from her lips.

And how Castor set off in search of him a few days later.

Ursula's stomach twisted at the memory of Raven attacking Castor. She loved them both and it had been awful to see them fighting. Raven trying to hit Castor and Castor trying not to get hurt or to hurt his twin.

70

Her tongue was still throbbing, and her head ached. She felt as if a tide of hot tears were making her eyes swell in her skull.

She handed Meer to Bircha, who was always happy to stroke the cat, and went in the direction Lupus had gone. She felt bad about their first meeting. She wanted to tell him she was sorry she had accused him of being cruel.

She was halfway to the brook when she realised she couldn't tell him because of her sore tongue.

Also, he was almost certainly bathing and she didn't want to come upon him unannounced. She was about to turn back when he emerged from some shrubs. His hair was tousled and his tunic damp. She guessed he had used it to dry his hair. They stood for a moment, looking at each other in the faint light of an almost full moon. Then he gestured towards the river, mimicked swimming and gave her a thumbs-up. She nodded and put her hands together, as if to say, *Forgive me?* He reached out, rested his hand on her head for a moment and then moved on.

But Ursula stood transfixed. His touch had sent a wave of warmth flowing through her, like the hot mulsum she had once drunk.

Instead of fading, the heat increased until she thought she could not stand it any longer. Stripping off her woollen tunic and dressed only in her nettle-cloth undertunic, she hurried to find the brook. It was scary putting a bare foot into ink-black water but the feel of cool mud between her toes was glorious. Taking courage, she plunged in. Instantly, the cold water sucked away the heat flowing through her.

Once she had watched a blacksmith put a red-hot knife blade into a bucket of water. The blade had hissed and steamed as it cooled.

She felt like that blade.

71

She imagined the steam rising off her as she went right under.

And when she came out an amazing thing had happened: for the first time in three days she could move her tongue without pain.

Chapter Eighteen
PHILOSOPHUS

It was early morning and they were only a mile from Viroconium when all movement on the road came to a halt. Something up ahead was causing a blockage.

Fronto and Vindex had been marching at the rear, but now they mounted their horses and rode forward along the grassy verge to see what was happening.

Clio and Silenos were in the driver's seat of the pantomime wagon and as Fronto and Vindex rode past, Clio called out.

'We have to be at the amphitheatre soon! We can't be late or we'll get off on the wrong foot with the troupe we're supposed to be joining.'

Fronto nodded to Clio and muttered to Vindex, 'I just hope it's not another hay wagon that's shed its load.'

'Or a flock of sheep like yesterday,' said Vindex with a grin. 'They're not so impressed by our swords and bows.'

It was neither hay nor sheep but a bearded old man in tattered robes and a walking stick.

'It looks like a philosopher,' said Fronto.

'A what?' asked Vindex with a frown.

'A philosopher. We used to have a lot of them in Rome. They would stand on street corners and in marketplaces and tell you how to live your life. Then Domitian banned them,' he added.

'He looks like a beggar.'

Fronto nodded. 'Some of them choose a life of poverty.'

'They choose to be poor?'

Fronto nodded again. 'They think it helps them concentrate on the important things in life.'

They were close enough now to hear what the man was saying. 'Repent!' The man was speaking in accented Latin. 'Turn from dark to light. Turn from the liar to the God!'

Fronto rode right up to the philosopher and looked down at him. 'I must ask you to get out of the road, sir,' he said.

The old man smiled up at him with swollen, red-rimmed eyes. 'I proclaim a new kingdom!' he cried. 'A kingdom of light and love and joy!'

Fronto swung off his mare. 'That is dangerous talk, old man.' He glanced around and lowered his voice. 'Don't let any Romans hear you preaching a new kingdom, or your life will be over. Now please move along.'

A tiny movement below the old man's mouth caught his eye and Fronto recoiled as he realised the philosopher's beard was infested with lice.

'Come on,' he said, gently putting a hand on the man's back. 'At least move over to the verge.' He could feel the man's knobbly backbone beneath thin robes as he guided him to the side of the road.

Vindex was making the crowd move to the opposite verge.

As Eros flicked the pantomime mules into movement, Clio jumped down off the wagon.

'Here, grandfather,' she said respectfully. 'Take this loaf of bread and this apple.'

The old man kept hold of the walking stick in his left hand

but grasped at the loaf with his right. He dropped it down the front of his tunic. The apple followed.

'Would you like to ride in our cart, grandfather?' Clio asked.

Standing behind the man, Fronto shook his head violently and mouthed the word: LICE!

But the old man was also shaking his head. 'No, I must walk and you must ride and all of us must bring the good news of the kingdom.' Still gripping his walking stick, he rested his filthy right hand on Clio's head. 'Bless you, my daughter,' he said. 'You have five trees in paradise which do not move in summer or in winter, and their leaves do not fall.'

Clio frowned, shrugged, then ran to catch up with the carriage.

As the others passed, the old philosopher proclaimed a message for some of them.

To Ursula, driving her chariot, he cried out, 'If those who lead you say unto you: behold, the kingdom is in heaven, then the birds of the heaven will be before you.'

To Bouda he said, 'Every woman who makes herself male will enter the kingdom of heaven.'

To Juba he said, 'Behold, the kingdom is within you, and it is outside of you. When you know yourself, then shall you be known, and you shall know that you are a son of the living Father. But if you do not know yourself, then you are drowned in poverty.'

When they were all safely past, Fronto swung back on to his horse. 'I warn you again, grandfather,' he said. 'Stop talking about this other kingdom, especially if it rivals that of Rome.'

The man was silent for a moment but as Fronto rode off he heard him shout, 'You cannot hide a light under a basket!'

Fronto shook his head. The old philosopher was obviously mad.

Chapter Nineteen
VIROCONIUM

Left by departing legions as a gift to the local people, Viroconium's small wooden amphitheatre was on the outskirts of town, near a tile factory.

As it loomed ahead, Fronto noticed people hurrying on foot across fields and along the side of the road.

'Head for that biggest entrance!' called Clio behind him, but as he and Vindex led the way towards the biggest entrance on the south, two soldiers stepped out in front of them. Fronto knew that Viroconium was now a civilian settlement and guessed the soldiers were from the nearest fortress.

He reined in his mount and gestured for the wagons behind him to stop.

'Lupus the Pantomime?' One of the soldiers consulted a wax tablet.

'That's us.' Fronto handed down their pass and prepared to get off his horse.

'No need to dismount,' said the officer. 'You're late enough as it is.' He opened the tablet, gave it a cursory glance, then inserted a slip of papyrus and snapped it shut. 'May I ask you to use the designated space on your left? Use the door marked "gladiators".' He gave back the tablet and pointed towards a staked-off approach leading to the west side of the arena. Two soldiers flanked this path.

Fronto nodded and led the others off to the left, past a sign reading PERFORMERS ONLY. He immediately saw two entrances on the side of the amphitheatre. The nearer one had the words GLADIATORES in red over it and the further was marked BESTIAE.

Fronto and Vindex duly led the others towards the door marked for gladiators. Although the entryway was high enough for Fronto to ride through, he dismounted so that he could touch the right-hand doorframe and step over with his right foot.

Inside, he was disappointed to see no gladiators, only a long dim room with stalls on the left, a bench on the right and a wooden gate at the far end. Judging from the bars of light filtering through the gate, he guessed the arena lay beyond.

Up above, the ceiling started lofty but got lower as they went in. Fronto realised the roof was formed by the seating.

'This isn't the sort of place we usually wait,' said Clio, looking around. 'But at least they've provided water and hay for the animals. Let's leave our team hitched,' she added. 'We might have to get away quickly to avoid Lupus's fans.'

Fronto left his horse in one of the stalls and went to the doors leading into the arena. A narrow horizontal slot at eye level showed him a sandy oval, raked and clean.

'The amphitheatre is already full!' he exclaimed.

'I thought the games weren't due to start until the sixth hour,' said Clio, coming up beside them with Lupus and the two musicians. 'Surely it's not midday already?'

A blare of trumpets made them jump. Fronto pulled the piece of papyrus out of his wax tablet. 'We were wrong!' he said.

'They start now. Look! Here's the programme!'

'Read it out loud?' said Bircha, looking at him with her big blue eyes.

Fronto nodded. '*Spectacle*,' he read. '*On the Nones of July. Sacrifice. Beast Hunt. Combat of Wolf versus Bear. Pantomime. Distribution of bread. Executions (if needed). Gladiatorial combats. Distribution of money. Conclusion. Events begin two hours before noon.*'

Another blare of trumpets brought their heads round and they crowded forward to peer through the narrow viewing slot.

'Greetings, citizens of Viroconium!' A tall Roman in a leek-green tunic moved into the centre of the arena. 'They say the name of your town means Place of the Man Wolf. This is most fitting! Today you will witness a battle between a bear and a wolf. You will watch the famous pantomime dancer Lupus, whose name means "wolf", and you will thrill to deadly gladiators from the Ludus Domitianus who are fiercer than any man or wolf!'

As the crowds above reacted, dust drifted down onto Fronto and the others. 'Don't stomp your feet!' the man shouted. 'Or the seating might collapse, as it did once in the time of Tiberius when more than thirty thousand people died!'

Almost as one, the two thousand pairs of feet ceased stomping.

Fronto made the sign against evil, and then spat on the straw-covered earth floor for good measure.

The tall man blared on, 'But first a sacrifice to the genius of our Princeps, so that the gods may bless our morning's entertainment!'

The sacrifice went well and the omens were favourable. As the helpers dragged the dead ram back out of the arena, some trumpets played a brassy fanfare and the man in leek-green announced the first beast fight. 'Three deer and a bear!' he said in a huge voice.

The applause was mixed with laughter and jeers.

Fronto also snorted, and glanced at Vindex. 'Deer and a bear?' He shook his head. 'In Rome I once saw a lion fight a rhinoceros.'

Vindex grinned. 'We're in the provinces now.'

A gate to their left swung open and three deer ran out on to the sand. A mixture of cheers and laughter greeted them. The terrified animals tried to return to their holding area, but the gate was already shut so they ran around the sandy oval, keeping close to the wall.

Ursula had been tending the pack animals at the back of their waiting area under the arena. Now she and Bircha ran to the viewing slot. Fronto moved over a little to let them see.

'Oh no!' cried Bircha. 'The poor deer! They have nowhere to hide!'

'*Nowhere to hide!*' echoed Loquax on Ursula's right shoulder.

Fronto knew that his sister and Bircha were both soft-hearted. 'Maybe you shouldn't watch this part,' he said.

'Oh!' gasped Bouda, who had come to watch, too. She pointed at the gate from which the deer had emerged.

Fronto took an involuntary step back as a brown bear entered the arena. It was not the sight of the shambling creature that set his stomach churning, but its rank smell.

'I thought you said you'd seen a lion fight,' remarked Vindex, his eyes smiling.

'I wasn't this close!' Fronto touched the wooden posts either sides of the slatted gate – *right, left, right* – for protection.

'That old bear is faster than he looks,' said Juba with a touch of admiration.

'*Find Jonathan!*' said Loquax.

Lupus guffawed and wrote on his wax tablet. JONATHAN ONCE DRESSED UP IN A BEAR SKIN.

Fronto nodded and turned back in time to see one of the deer skid to a halt in a spray of sand. To his amazement, the deer bowed before the seat of honour. The crowd gasped and applauded when – instead of attacking the deer – the bear left it unharmed and started for another. This deer also eluded him with clever tricks and bounds and when she knelt beside the first deer, the bear went after the third one.

By now the crowd was laughing and applauding. A great cheer went up when the bear brought down the third deer and began to feed on it.

When Ursula whimpered and backed away, Prasutus laughed.

'Even bears have to eat,' he said, taking her place beside Fronto at the viewing slot.

Bouda tipped her head for a better view. 'Who are those two deer kneeling before?'

'That's the tribunal, the president's seat,' said Fronto. 'The president or editor is a rich person who sponsors games because he wants to be popular. In Rome it's usually the Emperor who puts on games.'

'I wonder who's sponsoring these events?' asked Juba.

They heard a grunt and all turned to see Lupus holding up his wax tablet.

Fronto's eyes widened as he saw the name written there: DOMITIAN!

Chapter Twenty
BESTIAE

When Juba saw the name written on Lupus's wax tablet, his heart gave a cold thud.

'Domitian?' he gasped. 'Domitian is here?'

The words of the Emperor's edict were seared into his mind:

Wanted: children of the traitor Lucius Domitius Ursus and his wife Claudia Quarta, formerly of the Palatine Hill. The three children, two boys and a girl, have dusky skin and curly black hair and are possibly travelling with their baby sister. Their crime is treason and the theft of property belonging to the Princeps.

Juba looked at Fronto and knew that his brother feared the same thing: being caught by the Emperor's men.

'*Ave, Domitian!*' Loquax fluttered excitedly up from Ursula's shoulders.

If Juba pressed his face right up against the viewing slot, he could just make out the people sitting at the south end of the small amphitheatre above the main entrance.

He had never seen Domitian in the flesh, but almost every coin in his belt showed a portrait of the Emperor in profile. And once, in a palatial villa on the south coast of Britannia, he had come face-to-face with a life-sized painted sculpture. It had shown the Emperor's moist brown eyes, his weak chin and his sulky mouth.

'I don't see Domitian.' Juba frowned. 'Just a fat man in a broad-striped toga.'

'Don't worry,' came Clio's voice in his ear. 'Domitian is still in Rome. That fat man, Montanus, is his representative. They say Domitian gave him the choice of working in the mines or coming to Britannia to entertain Roman troops,' she added.

Juba turned his head. 'So Montanus isn't a friend of the Emperor?'

'He used to be,' said Clio. 'But not any more. Lupus would hardly be working with him if he were. Domitian is putting on all these shows to gain favour. Montanus is his representative and the thin man – Vegetus – is the announcer and organiser of all the events.'

Juba frowned. 'Remind me why you're travelling with a show sponsored by the Emperor?'

'Because we want to find Lupus's old friend Jonathan—' began Clio.

'*Find Jonathan!*' interrupted Loquax from Ursula's shoulder.

Clio lowered her voice. 'Because Jonathan has information that could end the tyrant's rule.'

Juba's frown deepened. 'Isn't it risky travelling with a show sponsored by the man we want to depose?'

'Shhh!' hissed Clio. 'But yes!'

Ursula was writing something on her wax tablet. She held it up: JONATHAN IS DOCTOR TO GLADIATORS! MAYBE HE IS HERE!

Clio gave a small frown. 'We're not certain, but we think Jonathan only treated gladiators when he was in Pergamum. Because he speaks Latin, Greek and Aramaic his patients would more likely be soldiers and auxiliaries than native Britons. After we perform here, this show is going to some of the biggest forts and fortresses in the province.'

Bircha frowned. 'What's the difference between a fortress and a fort again?' she asked.

Fronto answered. 'A fortress is a big camp full of legionaries, that is, citizen soldiers. Forts are smaller camps manned by auxiliaries such as Gauls or Germans.' Here he pointed at Vindex. 'And all auxiliaries have to be able to speak Latin.'

Clio nodded. 'Each time we arrive in a new place, Lupus and I plan to go to the camp doctor and ask for advice about his mouth. He gets ulcers, you see, from it being so dry. The doctors are always interested to see the effects of such a wound. While we are there, I casually ask if anyone has seen the man painted on the back of Lupus's wax tablet. Doctors are quite competitive and often know all their rivals.'

'That is a good plan,' said Prasutus.

'But why are *we* here?' asked Juba. 'What can we do to help?'

Lupus held up his tablet. YOU HAVE SEEN HIS MISSING NEPHEW IN THE FLESH.

'We think Jonathan is obsessed with finding Raven,' added Clio. 'Once he knows his nephew is safe he can turn his mind to other things. Like bringing down you-know-who.'

Lupus was adding a new message. ALSO, CHILDREN CAN SOMETIMES GO PLACES ADULTS CAN'T.

'Yes, I suppose that's true,' Juba admitted, turning back to study the Emperor's representative through the viewing slot in the doors.

Still, it was worrying to be so close to a man who wanted to win back the favour of their hated enemy.

Another cheer brought Juba's attention back to the arena.

The gate on their left had opened to release a big hound with shaggy fur in shades of grey and cinnamon.

'And now,' cried Vegetus, 'as promised, a savage wolf will battle a bear!'

Ursula gasped. She jostled Juba as she squeezed in for a better view.

Bircha cried, 'It's not a wolf! It's a segosa.'

'A hunting dog,' explained Bolianus. 'They hunt by smell.'

'We know,' said Juba. 'There were some at the village where we spent the winter.'

'It's not fair!' cried Bircha. 'How can a dog fight a bear?'

Wide-eyed, Ursula nodded her agreement and Juba saw her clench her fists so hard that her knuckles went white.

He tried to console them. 'The bear's been feeding on that deer. He won't be too fierce.'

They all watched as the bear lifted his bloody muzzle from the deer's red belly and stared with dull black eyes.

The dog-wolf ran straight towards him, then stopped a pace or two away and crouched in silence.

The bear stepped over the body of the deer to face the dog.

For a few long heartbeats the two animals circled each other.

'That's strange,' said Prasutus. 'Those dogs usually howl when they attack, in order to frighten their prey.'

'Maybe that one is too frightened to howl,' said Juba.

Ursula grunted and shook her head in disagreement.

As if to prove her right, the dog bravely leapt at the bear.

The crowd cheered and a few women screamed as the two great beasts rolled on the sandy arena.

'That's also strange,' muttered Juba. 'They seem to be wrestling, not biting . . .'

Like Juba, others in the audience were not convinced that

it was a real fight. Only a few people applauded. Most were shaking their heads or making rude noises.

Finally the two struggling beasts stopped wrestling. The dog lay still and the bear reared up on his hind legs. At the piercing sound of a bone whistle, the bear lifted his paws to his ears and revolved on the spot. His apparent victory dance made the audience laugh and there was a smattering of applause.

A big bald man with a squint moved forward. He held his whip in one hand and a victor's wreath in the other. The bone whistle was in his mouth.

'That's Polyphemus the beast trainer,' said Fronto. 'I heard one of the sentries mention him.'

Bouda said, 'He must be called that because he only has one eye, like the Cyclops, the giant in the *Odyssey*.'

Juba gave her an approving nod. He had been teaching her about Homer.

Accompanied by jeers as well as applause, the man called Polyphemus placed the wreath on the bear's head, then gave a smart crack of the whip and followed the bear back through the door from which he had first emerged. Six slave boys ran out. Two put the dead wolf-dog on a stretcher, two used hooks on ropes to drag the half-eaten body of the deer through one of the exits, while the last two boys raked clean sand over the bloody patches and put some bloody gobbets in a basket.

'That's strange,' Juba frowned. 'They used a stretcher for the dead dog rather than hooks . . .'

'Maybe he's only wounded, and not dead!' cried Bircha.

Ursula nodded, her eyes full of hope, and ran out of their holding area.

'*Find Jonathan!*' cried Loquax, flying after her.

Meanwhile, out on the freshly raked sand of the arena,

green-clad Vegetus mopped his forehead with a napkin. 'And now,' he proclaimed, 'Lupus the Pantomime and his troupe will perform the Myth of Actaeon, and I promise this time you will not be disappointed!'

He was right.

Fronto and Vindex pushed open the double doors to let Lupus and his troupe stride out on to the sand.

For the next half hour the people in the arena were utterly silent. And when Lupus took his final bow, they nearly brought down the wooden seating with their cheers and stamping.

Chapter Twenty-One
LUPUS

Ursula did not stay to watch Lupus's pantomime.

She had to see if the wolf-dog was still alive. Followed by flapping Loquax and with Meer on her shoulder, she ran out of the door marked GLADIATORES and into the wide doorway marked BESTIAE. With stalls, benches and hay, the dim space was like their area next door. But the stench of urine, wild animal droppings and fear made it feel completely different.

'*Find Jonathan!*' said Loquax. It was his new favourite phrase.

'*Meeer!*' Ursula's cat complained about the unpleasant smell.

Ursula's tongue was still swollen, so she reached up to her shoulder and stroked Meer's head in order to calm her.

She half expected to see the wolf-dog lying on the stretcher with people crouching over him, tending to his wounds. But the stretcher was propped against the wall by the doorway.

As her eyes adjusted to the dim light, she saw that the stalls contained animal cages.

She thought the first cage held the wolf-dog and ran to it. As she got nearer, a black creature threw himself at the wooden bars, snarling savagely.

'Ungh!' She jumped back. This was not the big cinnamon and grey hunting dog, it was a real wolf. And a ravenous one by the looks of him. His eyes were red, his dripping fangs bared and despite his black fur she could count every rib.

Even though he was in a sturdy cage, she backed cautiously away, her feet crunching on the smelly hay.

Now she could see that a cage in the furthest stall held the wolf-dog, apparently unharmed.

She ran past the caged deer and the sad-looking bear and went straight to the dog. Ursula half expected the female dog to begin howling mournfully as segosi usually did, but this hound only whined softly. She pressed her panting muzzle between wooden bars. Big brown eyes melted Ursula's heart.

Ursula bent down, let the big hound sniff the back of her hand and reached through the bars to stroke her. Then she felt something wet and sticky. When Ursula brought her hand out she saw that it was covered with blood. But the dog seemed unharmed.

They must use fake blood! It's all an act.

In her cage, the dog whined again softly, then panted with her big tongue, as if to say, *Please let me out?*

Ursula thought of dogs like this one who lived happily in the villages of the Britons, wandering in and out of roundhouses, howling for food or attention, sleeping in the sun, roaming the woods. It was cruel to cage them and force them to fight in silence.

She reached through the bars and gently scrabbled the top of the big dog's head. Ursula longed to be able to utter words of sympathy and tell her everything would be all right, but her swollen tongue would not allow it.

The dog's panting smile and trusting expression made Ursula want to cry.

She stood up and looked around.

The nearest cage held the bear and the one beyond the two deer.

When the bear saw her looking at him, he rose up on to his hind feet, put his forepaws up by his ears and turned on the spot. She could see some bald patches on his side with raw sores.

Meanwhile, the deer were banging against each other in terror, grunting and clattering against the bars of their cages.

Hot tears of outrage filled Ursula's eyes.

She looked towards the wide entryway. Bright light was coming in from outside but it barely reached this dark part of the structure. She knew there were green woods beyond the tile factory. She did not need to take a potion or chant magic words to know these poor animals longed to be free.

Where was their caretaker? Or the big, bald trainer called Polyphemus? She didn't know. All she knew was that, for the moment, the caged animals were unguarded.

And that whoever was in charge would be coming back soon.

'*Meeer?*' said Meer.

Ursula nodded, knowing that if she wanted to set them free it was now or never.

Chapter Twenty-Two
DAMA

Heart pounding, Ursula went to the deer's cage and quickly undid the latch. At first they did not want to leave, so she grabbed a small birch switch leaning against the wall and gently poked their haunches through the wooden bars. At last they came out of their cage, trembling and quivering. The deer took a few hesitant steps towards the light, then stopped.

She was about to smack them across the backside when the wolf snarled in his cage.

The deer bolted and Ursula watched their dark shapes head towards the light until it seemed to dissolve them. Next, she undid the latch of the dog's cage and let her out. The big hound butted Ursula's hand with her head and then licked it.

She gave her a quick hug, which the dog endured, panting with her big tongue. *I wish I could keep you,* she thought, *but you must go, too, dear segosa.*

'Go!' she commanded with her thick tongue, and pointed.

Obediently, the big dog trotted silently out of the dim cell and also vanished into the pure light of freedom.

Ursula waited a few heartbeats, until she thought the deer and dog were well away.

She glanced at the wolf cage, shook her head and hurried on

to the bear's cage. She knew bears could be dangerous but this one seemed utterly tame. And – unlike the starving wolf – it was well fed. Once again the creature put up his arms and turned on the spot, and once again his pathetic little dance made tears prick her eyes.

Ursula put the birch switch under her arm, for she needed both hands to undo the iron latch on his cage. As the door swung open, she hurried round to the back of his cage and smacked the bars.

The bear lumbered out of his cage, but instead of following the deer and the big dog out of the dim cell, he dropped to all fours and started sniffing at something in the rancid straw.

Ursula grunted 'Go!' as she had for the wolf-dog, but the bear ignored her.

She grunted again, '*GO!*'

The bear did not respond.

Finally, in desperation, she used the birch switch to flick at the bear's rump.

The bear turned and snarled at her. Ursula jumped back behind the bars of the open cage door.

'*Meeer!*' cried Meer and leapt from Ursula's shoulder into the shadows.

In their stalls, the two mules started braying in alarm.

The bear growled again and this upset the mules so much that one of them kicked the door of his stall with both hind feet. As the wood splintered, the mule charged out of his stall and out of the stables.

'Hey!' came a voice from outside. 'What's going on in here?'

Ursula dropped the switch and shrank back into the shadows.

'You boys get out of here!' came the voice again.

To her astonishment, Ursula saw two boys run past the main

91

entrance. They must have been lurking just outside.

A man's shape stood silhouetted by the bright square of the entryway.

It was the animal trainer, the man with the whip. He was a big man, bald and muscular. As he moved forward, Ursula caught a glimpse of the scarred eye-socket where his right eye should have been.

'And don't come back!' he cried over his shoulder. His voice sounded too light for his body.

The one-eyed man turned his good eye back into the depths of the gloom.

With a shudder, Ursula squeezed into the dark gap between two upright wooden beams. Her skin was dusky and if she closed her eyes maybe he wouldn't see the whites glimmer and she could remain unseen.

As he came closer she could smell his scent, a combination of lotus blossom and bear urine.

The sound of a whipcrack made her jump. 'Ursula!' he said in his strangely light voice. 'Get in the cage!'

Ursula gasped. Even with one eye and in this dim space the man had seen her.

Not only had he spotted her, but he knew her name.

Now this one-eyed monster was going to lock her in the cage with the bear.

Or maybe with the starving wolf!

Chapter Twenty-Three
URSA

'Get in the cage, Ursula!' commanded one-eyed Polyphemus in his boyish voice. 'Right now!'

In the dim animal cell beneath Viroconium's wooden amphitheatre, Ursula's heart was thudding so hard that she felt sick.

Could she make a run for it? No, was the answer. Not only was the big man blocking her exit, he had an ugly leather bullwhip in one hand.

'I said, get in!' he cried. 'Unless you want me to use this whip!'

She would have to brazen it out.

Venus, protect me! Ursula clutched the Venus down her front and mouthed the prayer, hoping the goddess would hear. Then she took a deep breath and stepped out of the shadows.

'*Eeeeek!*' The big man's shockingly shrill scream sent the bear blundering back into his cage.

Polyphemus the animal trainer made the sign against evil and then pressed his hand to the rough brown material over his heart. 'By Attis! You nearly sent my spirit down to Hades!' he said. 'What were you thinking, leaping out of the shadows like that?' He bent forward to peer at her. 'Where did you come from, anyway?'

Before she could form words with her swollen tongue, or even in her mind, he shook his head.

'Those bad boys let my animals out.' He shut the door of the bear's cage. 'Were they bothering you? Is that why you were hiding?'

For a moment Ursula didn't understand. Then she did. *He thinks the boys let out the animals!*

She breathed a sigh of relief and nodded. 'Yes,' she said thickly. 'Boys chase me. I hide here.'

Polyphemus looked around. 'I knew this sort of holding area was a bad idea. Usually you only have access via the arena, so the public can't get in and molest your animals.' He turned to the bear in the cage. 'Did those boys taunt you, Ursula?'

Ursula gasped as understanding flashed in her mind.

'Your bear . . . called Ursula?'

He nodded. 'It means little bear.'

'I know,' she said thickly. 'My name Ursula, too.'

He pointed at her. 'Your name is Ursula?'

She nodded.

He pondered this for a moment. Then a smile spread across his face. 'You thought I was asking *you* to go in the cage?'

Ursula nodded and laughed.

At the sound of her laughter, the bear named Ursula put her paws by her ears and turned in place.

'By Attis!' The beast trainer gasped and his single eye grew wide. 'She never does that for anyone. How did you do that?'

Ursula shrugged. 'I like animals,' she managed to say thickly. 'And they like me.'

'Wait!' He came closer, towering over her. 'Are you the girl everyone is talking about? You're with Lupus's troupe, right? They say you command panthers and ravens.'

As if on cue, Meer appeared from the shadows. A few leaps took her up to Ursula's shoulder where she sat purring.

'Not a panther, after all, I see!' The big man gave a grin, showing brown teeth. 'My name is Polyphemus. For obvious reasons.'

Ursula bowed and he bowed back. Then she took a step closer to the bear and pointed. 'Why sores?'

'She bites herself. And she won't let me put on the ointment.'

'Because small cage?'

'Not really,' said Polyphemus. 'She feels safer in a small cage. She bites herself more in a big cage.' He looked around. 'Those boys let my deer go. And Gartha, too. Thank Attis they didn't free the wolf.'

Ursula nodded and tried to look sad.

His good eye filled with tears. 'Gartha I can get back' – here he put two fingers in his mouth and gave a shrill whistle – 'but it took me ages to tame those deer. They're probably dead by now.'

'Dead?' Ursula clapped her hand to her mouth.

He nodded. 'If they go into the streets, people will kill them and eat them. They call it venison.'

'Won't they run to woods?' Ursula's tongue was beginning to ache.

He shook his head sadly. 'They wouldn't know how to survive in the woods,' he said. 'I raised them from babies.'

Ursula pointed at the bear in her cage. 'But she killed deer!'

'Oh, Ursula knows not to hurt Artemis or Diana. She always eats the third deer which we get especially for the show. That's always a wild deer.'

Ursula felt terrible.

She had tried to free the animals but had probably only succeeded in getting them killed.

Chapter Twenty-Four
SEGOSA

Ursula blinked back tears.

It was all her fault that the tame deer called Artemis and Diana would end up as someone's dinner.

When would she learn not to meddle?

But a moment later, big Polyphemus clapped his hands and pointed as the light in the dim cell grew even dimmer. The big scent-hound had returned, driving the two skittish deer before her!

Ursula clapped her hands, too.

'Gartha!' Polyphemus cried. 'Good girl!' Gartha stood on her hind legs, put her paws on his shoulders and licked his face. She was uttering a strange wheezy whine.

'Poor Gartha can neither bark nor howl,' explained the one-eyed trainer. 'Someone tried to kill her once but only succeeded in killing her voice.'

Ursula nodded sympathetically and gave Gartha a stroke or two.

The deer were still free, so Polyphemus moved to block the exit with his body and tried to push them into their cage.

'Now I just need to get Roseus,' he said. 'People will kill a mule for food and call it steak.' He stopped herding the deer for a moment and hung his big head. 'If only Faustus were still alive.'

'Who?' Ursula grunted.

'My assistant. He scratched his leg on a rusty nail last spring. It festered and he died on the Kalends of this month.'

Ursula had found the birch switch she'd dropped earlier and had just tapped the other deer in. Her tongue was throbbing again but she cried, 'I could be assistant!'

'You? Be my assistant?' He pursed his lips and then shook his big head. 'I don't think a girl could do it.'

'If I bring back Roseus, will you let me be your helper?' It was the longest sentence she had spoken in four days.

'*Meeer!*' said Meer.

'*Carpe diem!*' Loquax flapped down from above.

Polyphemus narrowed his single eye at her for a long moment.

Then, 'Yes.' He gave a single nod. 'If you can bring back Roseus unharmed, you can be my assistant.'

With Meer on her shoulder and Loquax fluttering about her head, Ursula ran outside. The fence to the tile-making factory had been knocked down and Roseus stood hee-hawing in the centre of a field spread with drying slabs of clay. Some workers were shaking their fists at the mule and cursing in Brittonic. Others were tugging their hair.

Ursula stepped over the broken fence, and picked her way among the leathery tiles. She gestured to the workers to be quiet and stand back. Thankfully, they obeyed.

As she got closer to the mule, he stopped braying. But he switched his tail and shook his head. Ursula stood still as a statue, not facing the mule directly but presenting him with her profile. The moment he twisted his ears towards her she turned her head, caught his gaze and held it exactly as she had with

97

mouse, cat and bird. Instead of sending her soul into him she called him silently to her. Then she calmly turned and walked slowly back to the amphitheatre.

Ursula's heart soared as the sound of his hooves told her he was following.

Her gaze still held power!

As she led Roseus back to the amphitheatre she saw why the workers were so upset, and had to lower her head to hide a smile. The drying tiles now bore the double-slotted footprints of two dainty deer, the fourfold pawprints of a giant hound and the lumpy hoofprints of an unshod mule.

Chapter Twenty-Five
DEVA

Fronto was disappointed when the soldiers told them they had to vacate their area immediately.

'But we haven't seen the gladiators,' he protested.

'They need the whole of this space to prepare,' the officer explained. 'That's why it's marked GLADIATORES.'

'Don't be downcast, Fronto,' said Clio as they rode out of the amphitheatre. 'You'll see the gladiators at Deva. We often leave early to get a head start,' she added. 'It helps us avoid the crowds. And look!' She pointed. 'The wild animals are coming with us!'

Fronto glanced back and grinned to see a wagon with cages driven by Ursula, with Polyphemus beside her and the big wolf-dog running beside it.

Their little convoy was on the road before the show had even finished. As they left the vineyards and fort of Viroconium behind, they could hear the crowds cheering even above the sound of wheels and hoofbeats.

That night they camped at a place called Mediolanum.

When they arrived at Deva the following afternoon, they were shown to quarters near the south entrance of the amphitheatre overlooking the river below. Their dormitory had stalls for the animals and bunk beds for the humans. Like the barracks at Isca

Augusta, where Fronto had trained, there was a columned porch outside with a brazier for cooking and also warmth.

They were going to stay here in Deva for the next two nights, so at last Fronto could watch the gladiator combats.

Early the next morning, when they entered the amphitheatre through the south entrance, leek-green Vegetus was there to greet them. As soon as he saw pretty Bouda and Bircha he asked them to dress up in order to toss fresh rolls to those on the lowest levels between acts. Fronto knew valuable prizes were sometimes scattered among the crowds at the games in Rome, but here in the provinces bread would have to do.

'Panem et circences,' he whispered to Vindex. 'Bread and games.'

'What?'

'Give the people free food and entertainment and they will love you forever. According to one of our poets,' Fronto added.

'This is our first event for an audience of soldiers,' Vegetus concluded his briefing. 'They're a hard crowd to please. Good luck!'

The sacrifice and Lupus's pantomime act were a success, but the beast fight between bear and scent-hound received more boos than cheers.

But the whole amphitheatre cheered when the gladiators entered for their procession.

'Dra-co! *Dra-co! DRA-CO!*' cried the men, and stamped their feet.

The bright note of a trumpet cut through the chanting and brought the stamping to a halt, though the crowd was still buzzing.

'At last!' said Juba, echoing Fronto's thoughts. 'Who's up first?'

'Celer the secutor will fight Falco the retiarius.' Bouda came in with an empty basket and flushed cheeks. 'The second bout will be Draco the murmillo versus Ajax the Thracian. Then winners of those bouts will battle each other.'

'Who told you?' Fronto asked.

'I saw the board when they were giving us the bread rolls to throw.'

Bouda and Bircha had just got back from tossing poppyseed rolls to the audience. They were dressed in long stripy tunics of blue and cream with flowered garlands. Bouda's cheeks were pink with excitement, but Bircha's skin was very pale. She had come to stand close to Fronto. The smell of her flowered garland made him a little dizzy.

'*I'm not scared, I'm excited!*' Ursula's bird fluttered down on to Bircha's shoulder and quoted a motto that Fronto had often used to give himself courage in the days before he was a soldier. He felt his face flush and glanced over at Bircha beside him. But her eyes were on the gladiators marching out into the arena.

'Oh!' Bircha gasped. 'Two of them are naked!'

'They're not naked,' Fronto pointed out. 'They're wearing loincloths.'

'*Loincloths!*' echoed Loquax and flew off again.

'Not very big ones!' Bircha covered her face with slender hands, but Fronto could see her peeking through her fingers.

'They're fat!' exclaimed Bolianus in surprise. 'I thought gladiators would be very strong and muscular.'

'They're not really fat,' said Juba. 'Just stocky.'

Fronto nodded. 'That layer of fat protects their muscles from minor cuts and slashes.'

Bircha looked up at him with wide blue eyes. 'Will they kill each other?'

'No, silly,' replied Bouda, who was standing on Fronto's left. 'They're too expensive.'

101

Fronto looked at her in surprise. 'You know about gladiators?'

Bouda nodded. 'In Londinium, if our gang had a good week cutting purses, Tyrannus took us all to the games. Some of his bodyguards were freed gladiators,' she added. She looked at Bircha. 'Don't worry; they don't die as much as you'd think. They even have their own personal doctor!'

Fronto wondered if Jonathan might be the doctor attached to this troupe. He was about to say something when a blare of trumpets announced the start of the first bout.

'Shhh!' hissed Bolianus. 'They're starting!'

They all turned to watch the referee draw a big circle in the sand. Then he put the tip of his rod in the centre of this circle.

The secutor and retiarius stepped into the circle, one either side of his rod.

The secutor, Celer, had padding on his left leg and right arm and wore a tight helmet with two small round holes for his eyes. He carried a sword and a big rectangular shield. The retiarius, Falco, had no helmet or shield. His only defence was his padded left arm with a metal flange at the shoulder and the thick leather belt above his loincloth. His weapons were a net, a trident and a small dagger in his belt.

When they were both in the circle, the trainer tapped the space between them with his staff and jumped lightly back.

For a few moments the two men circled each other. Then Celer the secutor jabbed his sword forward, fast as a cobra strike. The crowd gasped as Falco the net-man jumped back just in time. Now everything was motion as the net-man ran around the secutor, prodding him first here and then there with his trident and making Celer dance and slash in vain.

'The retiarius isn't very good,' said Bolianus. 'At that distance he should be able to stab Celer easily.'

'It's not about a quick kill . . .' said Juba.

'It's about entertainment . . .' said Bouda.

'. . . and making it last,' they said together. Fronto felt a pang of jealousy as beautiful Bouda smiled at his brother. But he forgot it when he felt a touch on his hand.

'How can the man in the egg helmet see?' Bircha asked him. 'He only has two little eye holes!'

'Good question.' Fronto smiled down at her. 'It's very difficult.'

'Oh!' cried ten thousand voices as one, and Fronto looked over to see the net-man's white loincloth blossoming with red.

As blood dripped down the net-man's thighs, pretty Bircha slumped against him in a partial faint. Fronto managed to catch her with his right arm. He was glad that he was wearing a small cloak so that his fish-scale armour wouldn't hurt her tender skin.

After a minute Bircha revived but then hid her face in his cloaked shoulder.

Fronto didn't know whether to look down at her or at the battling men. In the end he compromised by putting his arm more tightly around her while watching the gladiators.

The men fought on for perhaps another tenth of an hour, but it was clear that Falco the net-man was weakened by loss of blood. Once he managed to strike Celer's padded armguard with his trident and three dots of red appeared, but in the end Falco slumped to one knee on the sand and lifted his right forefinger.

'What is he doing?' asked Bircha in a small voice; she had turned her head to look.

'He's saying he's had enough,' explained Fronto. 'He's asking for mercy.'

All over the arena, men who had been chanting for Falco a quarter of an hour before were now crying out for his blood.

'*Iugula!*' they shouted, jabbing thumbs or making slicing motions. 'Cut his throat!'

Only a few people were waving napkins to show they wanted mercy. And so, when fat Montanus stood and pronounced '*Mitte!*' the crowd booed and jeered.

Montanus leaned forward in his throne and said something to green Vegetus down on the sand below.

Vegetus nodded and walked to the centre of the arena.

'Do you want blood?' he cried, throwing up both arms.

'Yes!' roared the crowd.

'Do you want death?'

'YES!'

'Then you shall have it.' Cheers filled the arena as he gestured to some slave boys who began to sweep away sand in the centre of the arena. They were uncovering a block of stone with an iron chain attached.

'What's that for?' asked Bircha. Fronto could feel her slender body trembling against him.

'No idea,' said Juba, and Bouda shrugged.

But Fronto swallowed hard.

Bircha was looking up at him with her innocent blue eyes. 'You know, don't you?' she said.

Fronto nodded. His heart was thudding and he felt sick.

'What is it?' asked Bolianus. 'Is it something bad?'

'Yes,' said Fronto. 'Something very bad. Come.' He took Bircha's hand and gently led her towards the back of the cell where their wagons were parked. He opened the back door of their white carruca. 'Go inside,' he said. 'Close your eyes, put your fingers in your ears and sing yourself a song. Don't come out until I tell you it's safe.'

Chapter Twenty-Six
DEFECTIO

Ursula frowned as she came through a small door that led from the beast cell to the pantomime cell.

'Ursula! What are you doing here?' Fronto's fish-scale armour glittered as he strode towards her out of the gloom.

Her brother's sharp tone made her stop in her tracks.

'Polyphemus.' She spoke slowly with her still-swollen tongue. 'He told me not to watch. He told me to go to you.'

'Quite right.' Fronto's expression softened. 'I've just put Bircha in the carruca. You should join her there.'

Ursula shook her head defiantly, opened her mouth to speak, then wrote on her wax tablet instead. DOCTOR JONATHAN NOT HERE, she wrote, BUT I FOUND OUT SOMETHING ELSE!

'What?' asked Fronto. He seemed distracted and kept looking towards the arena. She guessed he was more interested in the next bout than in what she had to tell him and so she wrote with satisfaction:

THEY USE FAKE BLOOD. IT'S ALL PRETEND!

'What?' That had got his attention.

The others came over. When they saw what she had written they all stared at her.

'Really?' Fronto raised his eyebrows 'The gladiators pretend to wound each other?'

'Yes,' she said, and wrote, THEY USE SAUSAGE SKINS FILLED WITH BLOOD FROM THE RAM SACRIFICE.

'That's cowardly,' Juba muttered.

'Not really.' Fronto stroked his chin thoughtfully. 'I imagine they still get lots of bumps and bruises and sometimes even real cuts. You can hurt yourself badly even in training. Also,' he added, 'it costs a fortune to replace a gladiator.'

Ursula moved closer to the gate. She pointed at the stone block and cocked her head in puzzlement. 'What's that?'

Fronto took a deep breath. 'I hope I'm wrong,' he began, 'but I think it's for—'

'An execution!' blared Vegetus. 'Before our final bout between Celer the secutor and Draco the murmillo, we will have an execution!'

Out on the sand, Vegetus opened his wax tablet. 'Certain professions,' he said in a huge voice, 'have been outlawed by our divine leader and Princeps Domitian. These include astrologers, diviners and augurs not officially appointed by Rome. Nor will philosophers, exorcists and magicians be tolerated, or members of cults that stir up dissent and insurrection.'

Ursula shuddered as she remembered the Druid cloak and sickle hidden in the carruca. With a trembling hand she wrote, WHAT IS INSURRECTION?

'It means anybody who goes against the order of things,' Fronto explained. 'Especially the Emperor.'

'But what is the block of marble for?'

'They chain the criminal to it, so he can't run away.

Everyone cheered, but Ursula's blood ran cold as she saw two soldiers bringing out the criminal. It was a white-bearded old man wearing nothing but a linen loincloth and iron shackles. His face, neck, arms and lower legs were brown in comparison with his pale torso. Bloody welts on his back showed that he had been flogged.

'Oh!' gasped Ursula, putting her cold fingers to her hot cheeks. 'It's that strange old man we saw on the road!'

Chapter Twenty-Seven
CHRISTIANUS

Ursula stared at the white-bearded old man, wondering what terrible crime he had committed.

'This man,' blared Vegetus, 'has been found preaching a new kingdom. He will be given a chance to renounce his foul practices and swear allegiance to the Emperor Domitian. If he does so, he will be released. But if not, he will suffer death by wolf.'

Ursula shuddered as she thought of the skinny wolf with the hungry red eyes pacing his cage. That must be why Polyphemus had wanted her out of the way.

Juba gripped her arm so hard that it almost hurt. 'Ursula, when I tell you, close your eyes.'

Ursula pulled free and scowled at him.

'Please. Do as I ask.' Something about his tone of voice made her nod.

Soldiers had brought the old man to the block of stone and began to fix the chain to the shackles on his ankles.

'Theophorus of Antioch,' cried Vegetus, 'do you renounce your depraved superstition?'

The old man's white head was down and Ursula did not hear his answer. He was so skinny that she could count his ribs. She remembered that he had called out to her. Something about birds and the kingdom of heaven.

'Once again I ask you, Theophorus of Antioch, do you renounce your perverted beliefs?'

This time Ursula thought she saw the old man shake his head, but she could still not hear his reply.

'For a third and final time,' blared Vegetus, 'do you renounce Chrestus, your so-called god?'

At this, the old man raised his white head and looked around at them all. 'Let him who has grown rich be king,' he said in a loud voice, 'and let him who possesses power renounce it. As for me, I do not renounce my king Jesus Christ. I worship him and I will be with him in paradise this very day!'

'Then I can do nothing more for you,' cried Vegetus, 'and I condemn you to death by wolf.'

A ragged cheer rippled across the amphitheatre.

Vegetus bowed to the crowd and then hurried out of the arena. His leek-green tunic flapped as he disappeared through one of the far gates.

The two soldiers who had chained the prisoner also hurried out.

A few moments later the black wolf ran into the arena.

Ten thousand men gasped.

Then a buzz of excitement filled the great amphitheatre.

For a while, the wolf ran around the edge of the arena, hugging the wall. But as he passed one of the barred exits something darted out and then back, quick as a snake. The wolf yelped and Ursula caught a whiff of singed fur. Polyphemus must have poked the poor creature with a red-hot spear. The wolf turned to lick his flank once or twice, then snarled with confusion. Ursula could imagine the pain growing, as it did with burns. Now he was not only hungry, he was angry. He lifted his nose, then loped towards the chained man.

'Close your eyes, Ursula,' said Juba. 'You too, Bouda.'

Ursula closed her eyes and covered her face with her hands. But she could not hear anything and curiosity made her peep.

The old Christian man was kneeling on the sand. His skinny arms were raised and he was trembling violently, shouting something about his master and his spirit.

His last words came clearly. 'Lord, forgive them; they know not what they do!'

Then the wolf was on him.

And this time the blood wasn't fake.

Chapter Twenty-Eight
ARENA

'Today's show,' said Vegetus later that afternoon, 'was a disaster. Montanus is not happy.'

They had gathered on the bloodstained sand of Deva's empty amphitheatre to hear his address. For the first time they were all together: gladiators, beast hunters, pantomime dancers and helpers. Vegetus stood in the box of honour, surrounded by empty seats. In the aisles behind him a few slaves were sweeping up hazelnut shells and other litter.

Gartha the scent-hound sat on the sand beside Ursula, who had her cat and bird on each shoulder.

Vegetus folded his arms across his leek-green chest, tucked his chin down and glowered at Polyphemus. 'The bear and the "wolf-dog",' he said, 'didn't fool anybody. They didn't seem to be fighting; they seemed to be dancing. In fact, it might have been better if they *had* been dancing!'

The big trainer shuffled his feet in the sand. 'Sorry, boss,' he mumbled.

Vegetus nodded and consulted his wax tablet. 'I should also say that two days ago I had a strong complaint from the owner of a tile factory in Viroconium. He says you let out the beasts and that half their tiles now bear the imprint of deer, dogs, mules or all three. The odd paw print is considered lucky, but your mule ruined a dozen of them. I had to smooth his feathers with a small amphora of imported wine from my private store.'

'That wasn't my fault, boss. Some boys opened the bear cage and it spooked the mules. The stable doors weren't very strong and Roseus broke out.'

'Someone should have been guarding him,' said Vegetus. Here he pointed at Ursula and her brothers and friends. 'That's what you lot are here for. To lend a hand wherever you can.'

They all nodded and Ursula swallowed hard. She hoped he never discovered the real culprit.

'Lupus, you and your troupe were excellent as usual. Thank goodness we have you to contribute. You lot' – here Vegetus pointed at the gladiators – 'were fairly good, but anybody with experience could probably tell your bouts were rehearsed. And the men in these big fortresses are experienced. You've got to come up with some new moves. Make it more exciting. More unexpected.'

'How?' Draco's grizzled eyebrows came together in a frown. He was their trainer as well as a combatant.

Vegetus scowled. 'I don't know! Surprise me! Also' – here he lowered his voice – 'don't spill the fake blood until the proper moment. Ajax was bleeding before Draco got in his first blow in that last bout. Now I've lost my train of thought . . .' He frowned down at his wax tablet and then nodded. 'That's right: execution of criminals. That was the high point of the show. That old man died very bravely and almost everybody was in tears. That stuff is inspiring. As Seneca said, "It is not a question of dying earlier or later, but of dying well or badly."

'So keep your ears pricked for word of any criminals that need executing, especially Christians or Druids. If we can get

112

a nice group of them then we can make them fight each other with eyeless helmets.'

'Eyeless helmets?' Bircha whispered. 'How will they see each other?'

'They won't,' muttered Juba grimly. 'They just slash blindly at each other, maddened by pain.'

There was a grunt of disgust behind Ursula. She turned to see Lupus leaving through the southwest entrance.

'What's wrong with him?' Vegetus narrowed his eyes.

Clio looked up from stroking Issa. 'He probably needed the latrine,' she said, giving the organiser a sweet smile.

Vegetus looked at her for a long moment, then shrugged and nodded. 'Tomorrow we set off for Mamucium,' he said. 'Montanus and his entourage are staying with a rich salt merchant outside the fort at Condate, which is halfway. I have sent ahead to book you rooms at the Cockerel Tavern there. We'll get an early start the next day as our show is the following afternoon. As most of you know, we lost two gladiators to fever at the start of this tour. But I don't have funds to buy new ones. So if you have any ideas for making this show better,' he added, 'come see me.'

Suddenly he pointed at Ursula. 'Especially you, Animal Girl.'

Chapter Twenty-Nine
CONFESSIO

Later, after dinner, as everyone was preparing for bed, Ursula went out to say goodnight to the animals in their cages. Gartha whined and put an imploring paw on her arm.

'I wish I could stay with you, but I can't,' she whispered. Then, to her surprise, Meer jumped down from her shoulder and went into the big dog's cage. Gartha lowered her big head to sniff the cat. Then she wagged her long tail. Ursula left Meer curled up and purring between Gartha's big paws.

When she came out of the stables the sun was setting and she saw Lupus standing near a low wall. Coming closer, she saw that the balustrade marked the edge of a cliff overlooking a river to the south. There were ancient elms down below and their canopy was almost as high as they were. The sky to the west was full of orange and red clouds.

She stood next to Lupus, resting her forearms on the wall. 'Are you all right?' she asked.

He gave a half shrug, then shook his head. She could see that he was as thin as a hound, all sinew and muscle, with not a spare ounce of fat. His profile looked like a fierce warrior's, but his sea-green eyes were brimming.

'Are you upset about the old man?'

Lupus nodded again. Then he pulled out his wax tablet and wrote on it, pressing lightly.

I HOPE I WOULD DIE THAT BRAVELY.

She frowned. 'What do you mean?'

He glanced warily around, and then wrote, CLIO AND I ARE FOLLOWERS OF THE WAY.

She gasped. 'You're Christians?'

He nodded and put his forefinger to his lips. JONATHAN, TOO, he wrote.

'Your friend Jonathan, the one we're looking for? He's a Christian?'

'*Find Jonathan!*' Loquax said.

Lupus shrugged. HE USED TO BELIEVE.

'And Flavia Gemina?'

Lupus gave a rueful smile and shook his head.

Then a shadow passed over his eyes.

DON'T TELL ANYONE, he wrote. OR WE'LL END UP LIKE OLD MAN.

He rubbed it all out and wrote a kind of code on his tablet:

S A T O R
A R E P O
T E N E T
O P E R A
R O T A S

This one he did not rub out; he let Ursula study it. She knew the words meant something like *Arepo the seed-sower holds the wheels with his effort*, but she did not understand what the sentence meant.

Lupus used his forefinger to show her that it could be read backwards as well as forwards and up as well as down.

115

Her eyes widened at this revelation.

MOST PEOPLE THINK CHARM TO KEEP AWAY EVIL, he wrote.

He rubbed it all out and wrote again, BUT REALLY A SECRET SIGN TO OTHER FOLLOWERS OF THE WAY.

As he closed his tablet, Ursula saw the portrait painted on it. It showed a young man with dark hair and eyes, a square jaw and a serious expression.

She pointed at it and frowned. 'Who is that?'

He opened his tablet again. JONATHAN BEN MORDECAI, he wrote. THE PERSON WE ARE LOOKING FOR.

'Did you paint that?' she asked.

He nodded.

'It's very good.'

He shrugged and then wrote, JUST A GUESS.

Ursula frowned. 'Why is it just a guess?'

HAVEN'T SEEN HIM FOR OVER TEN YEARS, he wrote. LAST TIME I SAW HIM WAS IN EPHESUS AT THE WEDDING OF FLAVIA GEMINA.

'Ten years is a long time,' Ursula said. 'As long as I've been alive.'

Gazing out at the valley before them, Ursula wondered if Jonathan was also looking at that same sunset. That made her think of Castor, and she wondered if he had found his brother Raven. As always, whenever she thought of the twins, she touched the ivory Venus down the front of her tunic and prayed as hard as she could in her mind. *Please, Venus, protect Castor and help him find his long-lost brother Raven, and then bring them back to us. And help us find Jonathan, too.*

Lupus pointed at the sunset and gave a wistful smile.

THEY SAY RED CLOUDS AT DUSK, he wrote, BRING FAIR WEATHER IN THE MORNING.

But to Ursula the blood-red clouds seemed a very bad omen.

Chapter Thirty
TEMO

They left Deva on a bright summer morning full of birdsong and clopping hooves, but the death of the brave old prophet had cast a shadow on Ursula's mood.

Skylarks were exulting overhead and Loquax flew up to join them. Ursula shaded her eyes and looked up.

She imagined what their procession might look like from his lofty point of view.

Montanus and his entourage would be somewhere on the road behind them. She had heard that he rode in a blue carruca and sometimes made his gladiators carry him in a lavender litter.

The sound of soldiers marching brought Ursula back to earth with a jolt.

Everyone in Britannia knew that when you heard soldiers coming you made way for them. She and Prasutus steered their teams to the right-hand side of the road and let the ponies dip their heads to drink from the ditch that ran alongside it. Behind them, Juba and Bouda had reined in the carruca and she could see the painted face of Lupus's carriage staring back at her from up ahead.

Everyone took the opportunity to get out and stretch their legs while the soldiers passed by.

Only they didn't pass by.

As soon as their commander saw the two chariots at the side of the road he halted his men and rode over to them.

He was a red-faced man with bushy white eyebrows beneath his helmet. The sideways crest showed her he was a centurion. He looked down at them with a frown. 'Did you know war chariots like these are illegal and have been for thirty years? Do you have a permit?'

Ursula's heart beat faster. She had hidden the feathered Druid cloak, but it had not occurred to her that the chariots might attract attention.

'These aren't war chariots,' said Prasutus respectfully. 'They are part of our show. See?' He pointed at Lupus's pantomime wagon.

The centurion shifted in his saddle to look behind. When he saw the painted eyes staring back at him he made the sign against evil.

'We have a show in Mamucium the day after tomorrow,' said Ursula.

At that moment, Fronto and Vindex came trotting up from the rear. Fronto saluted the officer. 'This troupe is under the governor's protection,' he said. For a moment he fumbled at his belt. Then he handed over a wax tablet.

The centurion took the tablet, opened it and frowned. 'This mentions a pantomime troupe and helpers,' he said presently. 'It doesn't say anything about war chariots. How are these part of the show?'

Fronto and Vindex looked at each other and then at Juba, who had come over from the carruca.

Prasutus came to the rescue. He gestured at Ursula. 'We ride these chariots in the arena,' he said, 'and do tricks.'

'What tricks?' The centurion handed the wax tablet back to Fronto.

'Tricks like this,' said Prasutus. Quickly pulling off his sandals, he stepped up on to the pole between the two white ponies and ran along it. When he reached the yoke over the ponies' shoulders he jumped up and did a half turn, so when he landed he was facing them again. He ran lightly back.

Ursula saw the centurion's mouth hanging open.

'You do that while it's moving?' he asked. 'You and this girl?'

'Yes,' said Prasutus, his cheeks flushing slightly. He spread his arms in a dramatic flourish. 'Can't you see? We are barbarians. I am a red-haired Briton, and she is a brown-skinned Amazon.'

'Briton versus Amazon, eh? Running along the yoke pole of a moving chariot?' The centurion raised an eyebrow. 'That I'd like to see!'

Prasutus gave an apologetic shrug. 'Too bad you're heading away from Mamucium,' he said, gesturing to the west.

The centurion gave him a yellow-toothed smile. 'Oh, don't worry!' he said. 'I'm only taking the lads for a stroll and a night under the stars. We'll be back the day after tomorrow, just in time to see your little show.'

Chapter Thirty-One
SAL

The next morning found them at the Cockerel Tavern in Condate. They were not due to perform because it was a travelling day, but when Ursula and Prasutus rode their chariots out of the stables at daybreak in order to rehearse their new act, they found soldiers erecting wooden seating in the shadow of a small fort. One of the soldiers stopped working and beckoned them over to an arena of the whitest sand Ursula had ever seen.

'We are making it for you,' he said, spreading his hands. 'We are hoping you will put on a small show. See?' He bent down and picked up a handful of sand, then touched his tongue to it. 'We have very little sand here in Condate, but lots of salt!'

'The arena is made of salt?' Ursula's eyes grew wide. 'I love salt!'

'Good,' said the man. 'You practise now and give us a little show in an hour or two?'

'We have to be away by noon,' said Prasutus.

'You will be away by noon,' the soldier assured them.

Although Condate's arena was the smallest yet, the sparkling white salt floor was as smooth and flat as a velvet cushion.

She chose the team she was most used to, the blacks. Prasutus had advised Ursula not to look down at the pole, but to keep her eyes on her goal and trust her feet. So Ursula fixed her eyes on the curved piece of ash that rested on the ponies' dark shoulders. Prasutus called it a dorsal yoke.

Even when the ponies were moving in a circle, the pole remained straight and stable, although it moved up and down a little.

Ursula laughed in delight as she ran up it and back several times, her bare feet enjoying the smooth feel of polished ash. Once, she felt herself about to unbalance so she jumped off. When her feet touched the salt she rolled in a somersault as she had seen acrobats do.

Prasutus was beside her in a moment. 'Ursula! Are you all right? Are you crying?'

Ursula shook her head and salt drifted down. 'I'm laughing,' she said. 'That was so much fun!' Without even stopping to brush off the salt she ran to her chariot, flicked the reins and got her pair of blacks moving again.

'I stopped concentrating for a moment,' she called to Prasutus. 'That's why I fell off. It's easy if you just let your feet guide you.'

They made several more circuits and then practised describing double loops where they passed within inches of each other.

'See!' Prasutus cried, reining in his team. 'I knew you could do it!' His cheeks had a ruddy flush and his blue eyes were bright.

A small creature sped from the shadows beneath the wooden seating. It leapt up on to the low chariot bed and then scrambled up to Ursula's shoulder.

'*Meeer!*' the cat said indignantly.

Ursula laughed and Prasutus said, 'If only you could do it with her on your shoulder!'

'I can!' She flicked the team into movement; they knew the

path by now. As they trotted round the sparkling, snow-white circle, she looped the reins over the side arch of the chariot body and jumped up on to the pole.

Up she ran, with Meer clinging tight, then jumped up on to the yoke, feet apart. She jumped up and turned, landed on the yoke and then ran back down to the body of the chariot.

'*Meeer!*' said Meer, when she reined in the team next to Prasutus. A smattering of applause made them look up. Lupus and his troupe had come to sit on some of the finished seating.

Clio cupped her hands around her mouth. 'How did you train your cat to hang on like that?' she called.

Ursula's tongue did not hurt at all as she shouted back, 'On board ship!'

'*Carpe diem!*' Loquax flew down on to her other shoulder.

They were all staring at her with something like awe, even the great Lupus.

Prasutus spoke in Latin so Lupus and Clio could understand, 'If you could do the trick with your cat here and your bird here' – he pointed at her shoulders – 'and with your hound following as you throw balls, you'd be more popular than any gladiators!'

'Good idea about getting Gartha to follow us!' Ursula clapped her hands. 'But I don't know how to juggle.'

Lupus pointed at himself and gave an exaggerated nod, as if to say, *I do!*

'Will you teach us?' Ursula cried.

Lupus nodded enthusiastically. He vaulted off the back of the seating, ran to his painted wagon and brought back a basket of turnips. They were small and wizened, but perfect for juggling.

Standing on the glittering white arena on that cool summer

morning, Lupus taught Ursula and Prasutus to juggle first three, then four turnips.

By the time the sun topped the fortress wall, they had mastered the art and were ready to perform.

It was only a small fortress, and their presentation hardly more than a practice session, but the small amphitheatre was full of soldiers.

Just before they were about to go on, a man in leek-green appeared. It was Vegetus, the announcer.

'What are you doing?' he said. 'You should be on the road to Mamucium.'

'You told us to think of new acts,' said Ursula. 'We're just trying one out.'

'It's a comedy act of Briton versus Amazon,' said Prasutus. 'It includes tricks with chariots.'

'We'll be away by noon,' promised Juba.

Vegetus glanced over at the two chariots standing hitched and ready. Then he looked at the wooden fort, lit by the morning sun. Finally, he looked at the arena of sparkling salt and the packed seating around it. 'The soldiers made this for you?' he said.

'Yes,' said Ursula. 'We were just going to practise in a field, but this is better.'

'All right, then,' he said. 'Try out your act. They're mostly Batavians here, famous for having no sense of humour. If you can make more than two of them laugh, there's an aureus in it for each of you.'

Ursula never forgot that golden morning. Not because of the slanting golden light of the sun. Not because of the golden hair of so many of the soldiers who almost destroyed the seating with their joyful stomping. And not even because of the golden coin she and Prasutus each received from Vegetus.

But because of the golden glow of happiness that filled her from her heels to her curly hair as she rode, raced, juggled and played with ponies, cat, bird and hound.

Chapter Thirty-Two
MAMUCIUM

Made bold by her success as a chariot acrobat, Ursula suggested a variation on the beast fight between Gartha the scent-hound and Ursula the bear.

A joke made by Vegetus a few days earlier had given her an idea. She noticed the bear moving whenever Lupus's pantomime troupe played music, and Gartha was clever and eager to please. With the help of Polyphemus, and using bloody gobbets of venison as treats, they taught the bear and the dog a new trick.

They showed Vegetus her modified act the next morning in the empty arena of Mamucium.

Bolianus and Bircha stood waiting in the shadows with flute and tambourine. Ursula opened the bear's cage and then Gartha's. The two approached each other as they usually did, but when brother and sister began to play a tune, Gartha rose up on her hind feet. This made her almost as tall as the bear. The two of them pressed paws together and shuffled around in a kind of dance.

When Vegetus saw this, he laughed. 'The dance won't replace the fight, but can you have them do it at the end, instead of the pretend kill?'

'I think so,' said Polyphemus. 'As soon as the music starts, that is their signal to rise up and dance. But it will mean lots of practice.'

Bolianus said, 'Lupus has asked Bircha and me to join his troupe. His other musicians want to stay here in Mamucium.'

Vegetus frowned. 'How does that change things?'

'It doesn't.'

Vegetus nodded. 'We'll put the animal dance at the end of the deer hunt, then Animal Girl and her chariot act followed by Lupus the Pantomime. Executions if necessary and we'll finish with the gladiators as usual.'

The following day fat Montanus and thousands of soldiers clapped when bear and wolf-dog danced together.

The audience laughed to see Ursula and Prasutus pretend to battle each other as Amazon versus Briton. She wore leggings and an embroidered tunic and carried a small Cupid's bow that Lupus had found among his pantomime props.

Later, the men applauded wildly when Lupus and Clio and their two new musicians performed the Twelve Tasks of Hercules.

Ursula was just beginning to believe she could get used to life in the arena when she saw the slaves uncover a block with a chain, just like the one at Deva.

She shuddered as she watched two soldiers lead a skinny man with a dark beard across the sand. Apart from a loincloth and a skullcap, he was naked. Like the old Christian, he had been flogged. But unlike the tanned old prophet, his skin was pale all over, with a slight sheen, as if he were oiled for the baths. She couldn't help thinking of the twins, whose skin was also the colour of ivory, so she touched her Venus and whispered a prayer.

Vegetus came out to applause, and opened his wax tablet. Then he spoke in his big announcer's voice.

'Certain activities,' he said in a huge voice, 'have long been outlawed by the Emperor Domitian. These include all astrologers, diviners and augurs not officially appointed by Rome. Nor will philosophers, exorcists and magicians be tolerated, or members of cults that stir up dissent and insurrection.' He paused and then shouted, 'We have such a one today.'

The crowd cheered happily.

Vegetus took another lungful of air. 'I will give this man a chance to renounce his faith and swear obedience to Caesar Domitian. If he does so, he will be spared. If not, he will suffer death by bear!'

Most of the crowd cheered but Juba heard one man shout, 'Not that nice bear who just danced with the wolf?'

Ursula gasped and looked at Polyphemus. 'Ursula would never eat a person! Would she?'

Polyphemus looked grim. 'They rubbed the man with pig fat,' he said. 'And Big Ursula loves bacon.'

'Oh no!' Ursula grabbed the wooden bars of the gate and prayed out loud, 'Please Venus goddess of love, and Diana goddess of bears, please *do* something!'

Chapter Thirty-Three
IUDAEUS

The expectant hush in Mamucium's wooden arena made Ursula open her eyes. Would her prayers to Venus and Diana be answered?

Green-clad Vegetus had turned to the half-naked man chained to the execution block. Ursula could see the whip marks on his back. 'Gaius Julius Theodotus,' he cried in a voice that all could hear, 'do you renounce your depraved superstition?'

'Yes!' The bearded man nodded.

Vegetus had been turning away. Now he whirled to face the prisoner. 'You what?' he choked.

'I renounce my depraved superstition! I, Gaius Julius Theodotus, will worship Caesar Domitian!'

'Are you certain? Don't you want to die nobly for Chrestus Jesus?'

'No!' The young man's voice was clear and strong. 'I'm not a Christian. I'm a Jew. Unchain me and I'll worship the Emperor right here and right now.'

Vegetus stared at the Jew in consternation. He had obviously not expected this.

There was a smattering of applause but most of the crowd was jeering.

'Thank you, Diana and Venus!' breathed Ursula. She touched the little ivory Venus down the front of her tunic.

As she pressed her face between the bars of the gate to see what would happen next, she saw Vegetus looking around the arena in desperation. When he spotted her peering at him, he beckoned.

Ursula frowned and pointed at herself.

Vegetus nodded vigorously, beckoned again and then mimed someone driving a chariot.

Ursula turned. 'Prasutus! I think he wants us to do our chariot battle again!'

'I've just unhitched the whites,' said Prasutus. 'Only the blacks are ready.'

'Then bring me the black team,' she cried, 'and join me as soon as you can!' She turned back to Vegetus, gave an exaggerated nod and pointed at herself.

She could see relief flood the announcer's face. 'Gaius Julius Theodotus,' boomed Vegetus. 'As you have renounced your atheism, the goddess Epona will rescue you!'

The angry jeers were now mixed with applause and laughter.

'Oh!' gasped Ursula. 'He only wants me, I think.'

Prasutus nodded as he led the black team up to her.

As Ursula went to get up into the chariot, she almost tripped on Issa's red ball. She knew the goddess Epona was always shown with bird and dog, so she bent down and picked up the red ball.

Issa gave an indignant yap.

Clio looked up from tuning her lyre. 'What are you doing with Issa's ball?'

'I have an idea,' said Ursula, dropping the ball down the

130

front of her tunic. 'Keep hold of Issa, then let her go when I give the signal.'

Clio looked puzzled, but nodded. She put down her lyre and picked up the yapping lapdog.

'Meer!' Ursula cried. 'To me!' And she snapped her fingers for Loquax.

Grinning, Lupus pulled open one side of the gate and a grim-faced Juba pulled the other.

Ursula flicked the reins and a huge cheer greeted her as she rode out into the bright arena, a cat on one shoulder and her talking bird on the other.

She glanced over at the post to see Vegetus fumbling to unlock the chains around the young Jew. *Why hadn't he used a rope which he could have cut quickly? Because he wasn't expecting the criminal to repent*, she thought.

Knowing that she would have to divert the crowd's attention for a few moments, she made a slow circuit with one arm raised in greeting. A light wave of laughter rippled across the arena, and Ursula breathed a sigh of relief. Laughter always defused anger.

On the second circuit she ran up and down the yoke pole, her pets faithfully clinging to each shoulder. The crowd clapped and laughed, but she felt she needed something new.

On the third circuit she pulled out the red ball and held it up, then nodded to Clio. A moment later Issa burst out of the gate and charged across the arena, her little paws sending up puffs of sand.

The laughter and applause got louder.

Ursula ran back down to the body of the chariot, took the reins in her right hand and held the red ball tauntingly in her left.

Issa pelted behind her, yapping furiously.

Ursula grinned. Looking over her shoulder, she drove just too fast for Issa to catch up.

The crowd was now enjoying the sight of a small white dog pursuing the goddess Epona in her chariot. Sometimes Issa tried to jump up, but she was too plump, and the crowd roared as she fell back, got up, shook the sand off and doggedly resumed the chase.

Glancing over at the punishment stake, Ursula saw that the young Jew was finally free and Vegetus was beckoning her.

With a click of her tongue and a subtle movement of the reins, she steered the team towards the post.

'*Meeer!*' said Meer.

'*Carpe diem!*' cried Loquax.

'*Yap, yap, yap!*' barked Issa.

'Jump up behind me!' Ursula called to Theodotus as she raced towards him. But he only looked at her stupidly, his face as white as chalk. 'Then catch!' she cried, and tossed him the red leather ball as she swept past.

Reflex was stronger than reason; the stunned man caught Issa's beloved red leather ball. As Ursula wheeled her team for another pass she was gratified to see Issa now making for Theodotus.

'*Carpe diem!*' urged Loquax, and fluttered up into the air.

As if waking from a dream, Theodotus turned and stumbled after the chariot, with little Issa in pursuit.

The audience was going wild: cheering, laughing and stamping.

Even Ursula giggled at the sight of the half-naked man running away from the small dog and trying to get into the chariot. She had been planning to slow down and let him get up behind her, but she realised this was much better.

'Keep running after me,' she called to him over her shoulder. 'We're heading for that gate.'

And so, to thunderous applause, the goddess Epona and her cat drove out of the arena, pursued by a half-naked man, a talking bird and a yapping lap dog.

Chapter Thirty-Four
PHILOTIMEA

Juba could hardly bring himself to look at the half-naked man who had run into their preparation area beneath the wooden amphitheatre of Mamucium.

'Oh, thank you!' Theodotus gasped, falling to his knees on the hay-strewn floor. 'I thought it was the end.' Issa came up to him and dropped her ball. He laughed almost hysterically as she began to lick him. 'Good puppy!' He patted the top of her head.

Bircha rushed forward and put her own pale lavender cloak around the man. But Juba glared down at him.

'Get a hold of yourself,' he said. 'Aren't you ashamed?'

'Juba!' cried Bouda, handing the man a beaker of posca. 'The poor man almost died.'

'Better death than shame,' said Juba. He turned back to the man. 'You renounced your gods!'

The man drained the beaker and wiped his mouth with the back of his arm. 'I am ashamed and utterly humiliated,' he said, handing back the beaker and rising unsteadily to his feet. 'But I have a wife and four children to support. My God knows my heart. He would be angrier if I abandoned them.'

'But to run away like that!' Juba's heart was thumping and his hands were shaking almost as much as the Jew's.

Theodotus pulled the cloak around his shivering body. 'I'm already in trouble with my God: today is the Sabbath and I'm in the arena. But seriously, I'd rather run away than give my rival Nymphidius the satisfaction of seeing me die,' he said. 'I'm sure he gave them my name for the reward.'

'Reward?' said Bouda.

'Yes,' said Theodotus. 'They're offering a gold coin to anybody who turns in rebellious Druids, Christians or Jews. But I found the flaw in their plan. Not to be rebellious.'

As he began to giggle hysterically, Juba turned away in disgust.

Fronto came in. 'Your wife and children are waiting for you outside,' he said. 'They brought you these.' He handed the man a tunic and cloak. The tunic was patched and the cloak so thin that Juba could see the texture of the weave.

Theodotus pulled on his threadbare tunic and handed the lavender cloak back to Bircha. 'I'm afraid I got blood and pig grease on your lovely cloak.'

'No,' she said with a smile. 'Keep it.'

'Really?' The man looked up at Bircha. When she nodded, he reverently stroked the lavender cloak. 'This is made of the finest wool,' he murmured in wonder. 'It's worth a fortune! I don't know how I can thank you. If there is anything I can ever do . . .'

Lupus stepped forward, his wax tablet extended before him.

Theodotus stopped fumbling with the toggle at the neck of his new cloak. When he saw the portrait of Jonathan ben Mordecai, the last of the colour drained from his already pale face.

'Do you know him?' asked Juba sharply.

'Why?' The Jew's voice caught and he had to clear his throat. 'Do you intend to report him and get the reward?'

Lupus shook his head violently and Clio said, 'No! We want to help him. We have some good news for him.'

Theodotus reluctantly took the portrait and studied it. 'I'm not sure. Maybe it's not him.'

'Lupus did the painting by guesswork,' said Clio. 'He was friends with this man when they were boys. So it won't look exactly like him.'

Lupus pressed the palms of his hands together and looked beseechingly at the Jew.

'A few weeks ago I saw a doctor who looked like that—' He stopped, alarmed at Lupus's cry of triumph.

Clio smiled reassuringly. 'Don't worry. Lupus is happy because our friend is indeed a doctor. Tell us more.'

'I don't know much more,' said Theodotus. 'He was doing a demonstration. A surgery. Sewing up the leg of an injured legionary. There was a big crowd.'

'Do you remember his name?'

'Yes, it was something strange. Oh, I remember! He called himself Prometheus.'

'Oh, too bad,' said Ursula. 'It's not him after all.'

But Lupus gave a strangled cry. Then he pointed at Theodotus and nodded violently.

'His name *is* Prometheus?' said Juba.

Lupus waggled his hand and then nodded.

'Where was this?' said Fronto.

'In Eboracum,' said Theodotus. 'I'm a cheese merchant and I was there on business. He was doing the demonstration in the vicus just outside the fortress walls.'

Lupus clapped his hands and held up three fingers to Clio.

'Yes,' she said. 'We'll be there in three days.'

Clio gripped the man's hands. 'Thank you!' she said. 'You

can't imagine how much that means to us; knowing we might be able to find him in Eboracum.'

'I'm glad I could help,' said Theodotus. 'May I pass out now?'

'What?' said Juba.

But Theodotus had slumped on to the floor of the changing cell in a dead faint.

Chapter Thirty-Five
URTICAE

They set out with renewed hope before the show had finished and made camp at a place where the road started to climb. But Fronto's mind was in turmoil.

Once before he had been prepared to die to preserve his honour, but he kept wondering what he would do if he were chained to a block. Would he beg to be released? Or would he meet his end bravely?

As Fronto stood guard over the little camp, he pondered the Jew's dilemma. Even after Vindex relieved him and he crawled into their goatskin tent, the turmoil in his heart would not let him sleep.

At last he dropped off, and when he woke it was to the sounds of his friends breaking camp.

It was warm and stuffy inside the dim goatskin tent. Vindex had put the flap down so that the brilliant morning light would not wake him too early. When Fronto pushed it aside, sunlight flooded his eyes and made him squint. A cockerel's crowing told him a settlement was nearby and he heard the faint sound of a Roman horn calling reveille. So it wasn't so late after all.

The light of these British summer mornings still amazed

him. Even in sunny Italy he had never seen this much light this early. There was something despotic about it, like a commander telling him to get up and get busy.

Fronto grunted a good morning to Juba, Prasutus and Bolianus who were hitching the animals to the wagons and chariots. The black team were already in their harnesses and he saw Ursula crouched by one of the pony's feet, applying some kind of leaf poultice. The others were rolling up sleeping skins or coming back from the brook. Lupus was kicking earth over the campfire. He waved a greeting and silently handed Fronto something like a scroll. It was a piece of rolled-up flatbread, still faintly warm and with soft cheese inside. Fronto wasn't hungry yet, but he knew he might not have a chance to eat until later so he accepted it with thanks and ate it as he walked into the copse.

After relieving himself in the bushes, he went to the brook and splashed water on his face. When he came back he saw Bouda sitting in dappled sunlight, her copper head framed against a pale square. She was weaving on a small loom about half her height. 'What are you doing?' Fronto asked.

'I'm weaving.'

'Why?'

'I like it.' She turned to look up at him. As always, her green gaze made his breath catch. His father had once owned a pair of chrysolite gems that looked like her eyes. Fronto had been fascinated by the colour.

He realised he was staring and said, 'You *like* weaving? My sister Ursula hates it.'

Bouda turned back to finish the row she was working on. 'I like it,' she said. 'It helps me not to worry. I try to do it for an hour each morning. I enter a kind of trance, and when I come back my mind is clear and refreshed.'

Fronto nodded. 'I get that from marching,' he said.

She held up her hand to him.

For a moment, Fronto gaped like a fool.

'Help me up?' she said, her eyes smiling.

'Of course.' He pulled her to her feet. Her hand was smaller and stronger than he had expected.

'May I have my hand back now?' Her green eyes sparked with amusement.

'Oh!' Feeling foolish, he let go of her hand.

She put the loom under her right arm and picked up a rush basket with her left hand. The basket contained a ball of thick papyrus-coloured thread and something that looked like flax fluff.

'What is that?' He reached out his hand to touch the whey-coloured flax.

'Nettle,' she said.

Fronto jerked his hand back as if the fibre might burn his fingers.

Bouda laughed. 'It won't sting now,' she said. 'It's been retted, dried, split and carded.'

Fronto was amazed. 'You can make clothing from nettles?'

'Yes. It's very strong and soft. Even silky.' She held up the loom with its tight, half-woven web of fabric. 'Feel it.'

'It *is* silky!'

'And best of all,' she said, 'cloth made of nettles is apotropaic.'

'Apotropaic? You mean it keeps away evil?'

They had reached the back of the carruca. She climbed up into the open door and he saw her lift one of the bench covers and put the loom and basket inside.

She came back down into the sunlight. 'Yes. According to Bircha, cloth made from nettles keeps away evil. I'm going to make a lovely soft undertunic that will protect the wearer from all danger.'

Once again, Fronto gaped at her. He had been captivated by Bouda the first moment he saw her. It was her look of scorn that had made him join the army; he had wanted to become brave. For her.

Then he had met beautiful Bircha, with hair as pale as moonlight. She looked at him with her long-lashed blue eyes and fainted in his arms. Bouda made him aware of all his fears, whereas Bircha made him feel brave.

In that moment, he realised that although Bouda still captivated him, he really loved Bircha.

But what if Bouda had finally come to admire him, now that Bircha had made him brave?

What if the tunic was a love gift?

He swallowed hard. 'Who is the tunic for?'

Bouda tipped her head slightly and gave him an amused smile. 'Why, it's for you, Fronto. Who else?'

Chapter Thirty-Six
RES ILLICITAE

Now that Ursula's tongue was healed, she was happy to be on a quest for the mysterious Doctor Jonathan. For three days they had been crossing a ridge of mountains, so there were no games full of blood and death, but only life and birdsong and blue sky. She and Prasutus drove the chariots side by side. Gartha ran happily along beside her, Meer sat on her shoulder and Loquax fluttered overhead. As they clopped along the last stretch of road to Eboracum, she was not worried when their convoy was stopped by a cohort of Roman legionaries.

'Please dismount,' commanded a lean officer with pale blue eyes. 'We have orders to search all persons, pack animals and vehicles for banned goods.'

Fronto galloped up. 'What kind of banned goods?' he asked.

'Weapons, subversive letters and anything to do with illicit religions,' said the officer. 'Especially Druidism. The Emperor Domitian has heard reports of a possible resurgence of that unholy sect.'

Ursula stifled a gasp. *There were Druidic objects hidden in the carruca!*

'You don't need to search us,' said Vindex. 'We're on a mission for the governor.'

Fronto fished in his belt. 'Here's the letter with our orders.' He held out the document.

'Sorry,' said the officer. 'No exceptions. We have to search these vehicles. I would be most grateful if you would unpack your things and put them on the side of the road.'

Fronto and Vindex looked at each other and then dismounted.

Ursula's heart was racing.

Would they find the cormorant-feather cape she had hidden in the carruca? And there was also the small golden sickle she had recovered from a Druid's charred corpse!

She wanted to signal Fronto to distract the officer, so that she could hide the incriminating items under the straw in Big Ursula's cage, but it was too late.

The soldiers were already going into the carruca.

Maybe they wouldn't realise there was storage beneath the seats.

Her hopes were dashed as one of the soldiers emerged holding the padded seat cover of one bench and leaned it against the side of the carruca. They began to bring the stored items out on to the sunny road: their baskets of vegetables and animal feed, the dismantled loom, the strands of nettle-stalk, the three hunting javelins.

'Spears aren't allowed,' said one of the soldiers.

Prasutus stepped forward. 'Those are javelins for hunting.'

Juba added. 'You can see by the rust that we hardly ever use them.'

'Then you won't mind if we confiscate them.'

'No. Of course not,' said Fronto. Ursula noticed him secretly making the sign against evil behind his back.

The officer looked at him keenly and then at the others. 'Where are you from?' he said.

Fronto stood to attention. 'Beneficiarii of the governor, on secondment from the first cohort of Hamian Archers.'

'I ask,' said the officer, 'because you look like them.' He pointed at Ursula and Juba.

'We come from all over,' said Juba quickly. He pointed at Clio and Lupus, coming up from the rear. 'We're part of Lupus's pantomime troupe.'

'Ah!' said the officer. 'Lupus the famous pantomime.'

'Sir?' One of the legionaries emerged from behind the carruca. 'We found these.'

Ursula did not move her head, but she could see the glint of a golden sickle and the cormorant-feather cape.

'I'd call that a Druid ritual object,' said the officer, examining the sickle. 'Used for peeling the skin from Roman soldiers, or so I've heard!' He turned to Fronto and Vindex.

'Wait!' Ursula cried, her heart in her throat. 'Those are mine!'

The officer and his soldiers all stared at her.

'It's for one of our acts, isn't it Prasutus? Britons versus Druids!'

'I thought Druids *were* Britons,' said one of the soldiers. 'How can they be against each other?'

Prasutus ran his hand through his dark red hair. 'Because the good Britons want to wipe out the evil Druids.'

'Which one of you is the Druid, then?' frowned the officer, looking from Prasutus to Ursula and back.

'I am!' Ursula snapped her fingers, fished in her belt pouch and when Loquax fluttered down on to her right shoulder she gave him a crumb of cheese. 'I'm the *Druid*!' she said, emphasising the word Druid.

Loquax obligingly added, '*Druid in the Deathwoods!*'

'*Meeer!*' said Meer, not to be outdone.

'See?' said Ursula brightly. 'I command animals, like this fierce panther and this talking raven! And this wolf-dog!' She added as Gartha came bounding up.

'We're performing tomorrow,' said Prasutus. 'Come and see!'

'Wouldn't miss it for the world.' The commander raised an eyebrow. 'I assume it's not the same act as your Amazon versus Briton?'

'What do you mean?' stammered Ursula.

The commander held up a wax tablet. 'One of the auxiliary commanders sent me a report mentioning an act with chariots and bow and arrows. I presume this one is different?'

For a moment, Ursula's mind froze like a rabbit facing a lion. Then she gave the officer her most radiant smile, the one she had used on her father whenever he caught her climbing on the grape trellis or talking to the slaves.

'Of course it's different!' she cried.

But later that evening, over barley and carrot stew, she looked at the others with a churning stomach. 'How can we make it different?'

'I have an idea,' said Prasutus. They all turned to him. In the firelight his face seemed almost as ruddy as his hair. 'Instead of hatred,' he said, 'why don't we show love?'

Ursula's eyes widened. 'What do you mean?'

'I can pretend to be a savage British boy who falls in love with an animal-loving Druid girl.'

Bircha's silver-blonde hair gleamed as she leaned forward. 'What a good idea!' she said softly. 'We can show that Druids can be kind and gentle!'

Bouda gave Prasutus a keen look. 'Are you blushing, Prasutus?'

Before he could answer, Ursula clapped her hands. 'It's a

145

brilliant idea!' she said. 'The story of how the Druid girl tames animals, and then tames savage Britons. It might even make the Romans stop fearing Druids. We can ask Clio to sing the story!'

'I, too, think it's a brilliant idea,' puffed a voice in cultured Latin.

'Halt! Who goes there?' Fronto clanked to attention.

'It is I.' A fat man waddled into the firelight. 'Your patron, Montanus.'

Chapter Thirty-Seven
EBORACUM

Montanus was aptly named, first because his family came from the Italian Alps and second because he was the size of a mountain.

Although Ursula had seen him almost daily in his place of honour, that night on the road to Eboracum was the first time she had seen him up close.

The big patrician and his two slaves usually stayed in the luxurious commander's quarters at the heart of each fortress.

The rest of them had to stay wherever they were put: an unused barrack near a stable or an inn outside the fortress. Including the eight gladiators, their troupe consisted of over twenty people, a dozen draft animals and as many as six performing beasts.

This evening, Montanus was accompanied by his two slaves. He was obviously unused to walking, for he was breathing hard. 'I loved your Amazon versus Briton act in Mamucium,' he said to Ursula. 'And the finale of the bear and hound combat was surprisingly poignant. So I am very happy for you to try out your Savage Briton tamed by a Druid Maiden act tomorrow. No, no,' he waved away the folding chair that Lupus had run to bring. 'I must get back to my wagon. I fear I won't sleep a moment,' he added. 'I'm used to a real bed, not a couch in a carriage. But necessity must be honoured.'

The following afternoon in Eboracum, Montanus personally addressed the soldiers for the first time in two weeks.

'The Emperor Domitian,' he puffed, 'wants you to know how much he appreciates your service. I hope you enjoy our little show.'

When it came time for their new act, Ursula emerged from the western arch beneath the seating, driving her team of black ponies. She was wearing her wine-red woollen tunic and her green-black feathered cape. The sickle hung on a cord around her neck, where all could see it gleam against her tunic. She had put two feathers in her long hair, which she wore loose, the black tendrils flying out behind as she urged the ponies forward at speed.

As Ursula made her circuits, Clio sang of how there were good Druids as well as evil, and that the good ones loved trees, animals and, above all, peace. She sang that they used their chariots for play, not war. This was Ursula's cue to run up along the pole of the chariot and then back.

The crowd loved this but applauded even more enthusiastically when a cat scampered across the sand, leapt on to the chariot and scrabbled up to Ursula's shoulder. This was a more difficult feat than normal because, unlike her cloak, the cape of cormorant feathers was slippery.

Laughter echoed across the amphitheatre as a small white dog with a mistletoe collar ran out and joined the girl Druid on her chariot. When the applause was dying down, Prasutus drove into the arena. With his bare skin painted blue and his shoulder-length red hair streaming out behind him, he cut a striking figure. As he did his first circuit, he brandished a painted wooden sword and roared at the crowd.

'One day,' sang Clio, 'a warlike Briton came back, fresh from chopping Batavian heads.'

Without slowing the chariot, Prasutus put the sword in the belt of his loincloth, looped the reins around the side arches of the chariot and bent down. When he stood upright again the crowd gasped, for he was holding four blonde heads, two in each fist. A few women screamed, but the soldiers laughed; they could see that the heads were sewn from white linen and yellow yarn, with the eyes and mouths embroidered in black and red.

Ursula drove her chariot behind his, knowing that this would keep his white team moving.

Balancing on the body of his fast-moving chariot, Prasutus juggled the heads. The crowd clapped and cheered.

When Prasutus went up on to his chariot pole, still juggling, the crowd went wild, stamping their approval.

'Then the warlike Briton caught sight of the peace-loving Druid girl,' sang Clio.

At this, Ursula overtook his slowing chariot and he pretended to notice her for the first time. As she passed, she gave him a smile so dazzling that it could be seen in the highest seats.

'The fierce Briton renounced the prizes of Mars' – here Prasutus tossed the heads behind him on to the sand – 'in favour of a prize more fitting to Venus!'

Now came the part they had only practised once or twice.

Ursula had to let herself be snatched up without harming the animals, but also ensuring that they came with her. She quickly reached down and plucked the slippery red ball from Issa's mouth.

And not an instant too soon, as a muscular arm swept round her waist. One moment she was in her chariot and the next she was breathlessly bouncing beside Prasutus in his.

Loquax flew up in alarm and Meer dug her tiny claws in so deep that Ursula gasped.

For a few heartbeats, it felt real. She caught a whiff of Prasutus's scent, the tang of sweat mixed with sweet oil from the baths. She could feel his heart beating hard against her left shoulder blade, even through the triple layer of tunics and feathered cape.

Meanwhile, Issa had jumped down from the abandoned chariot and was now scampering behind, uttering a yap so high and insistent that it could even be heard above the laughter.

Ursula was laughing, too, when something struck her side: something huge and furry and panting. She was falling, and Meer was yowling, but a strong arm was still round her and when they came crashing down on to the sandy arena, Prasutus broke her fall with his body.

For a moment she lay like a beached fish, mouth open as she tried to catch her breath. When it finally came back in a great gasp, her first thought was for her cat.

'Meer?' she cried and sat up. Meer was standing a short distance away, her little back arched and her fur standing on end. She was looking at something behind Ursula.

Ursula turned and gasped. Prasutus was lying on his back in the sand, with the giant jaws of Gartha the hound clamped around his neck.

Chapter Thirty-Eight
ADVENTUS

'Gartha!' cried Ursula. 'Get off Prasutus! He wasn't attacking me! It's part of our act!' Then she remembered the dog obeyed Latin commands, so she called again in Latin. 'Gartha! Come!' This time the big hound responded. She lifted her head and backed away, but did not take her eyes from Prasutus.

'Prasutus!' Ursula scrambled across the sand to him. 'Did she bite you?'

'I'm not sure,' he said without moving. 'It doesn't hurt but I feel something warm and wet.'

Ursula touched his neck and laughed with relief. 'It's only slobber,' she said. 'Gartha didn't even break your skin.'

She was aware of the crowd chanting, so she stood up and stretched out her hand to him. She had to use all her strength to help him up.

'Just give me a moment,' he muttered. 'I'm not sure my knees will hold me. Pretend to hug me.'

She gave him a pretend hug and could feel him shivering. The crowds cheered when Gartha butted up between them. And when she wagged her tail, they laughed. Not to be left out, Meer jumped up on Ursula's shoulder and Loquax landed on her head.

Prasutus laughed. 'I can't compete with all your animals,'

he said, pulling back. 'Shall we exit together? Each in our own chariots, but maybe still holding hands?'

And so, a few moments later, they mounted their chariots and rode out of the arena holding hands and with the dogs following.

People were applauding but she could also hear some calling for the gladiators.

She sighed and shrugged. After all, the gladiators were the main event.

Once in the dim refuge of their allotted space beneath the seating of the great amphitheatre, Ursula jumped down from her chariot and threw her arms round Gartha's furry neck. 'Thank you for looking after me,' she whispered. 'And thank you for not killing Prasutus.'

'He was never in danger.' Polyphemus tossed Gartha her marrowbone from the morning sacrifice. He set down a small bowl of milk for Meer and a raisin cake for Issa. 'Gartha was originally trained as a lady's bodyguard. She won't kill unless you say the word "kill" in Latin.'

Ursula looked up. 'Why did her mistress sell her to you?'

Polyphemus shook his head sadly. 'The lady's husband sold her,' he said, 'because his wife died of fever. Even Gartha couldn't protect her from that, could you, old girl?' He patted the dog's head. 'The husband was so grief-stricken that he tried to kill her by cutting her throat. But she's a tough old girl. She survived.'

Ursula's heart melted for Gartha.

As Prasutus came to sit beside her, Ursula felt a huge surge of affection for him, too.

'Oh, Prasutus!' she cried. 'I thought for a moment that I'd lost you.' Impulsively she threw her arms round him.

Prasutus laughed. 'I guess that's the last time we'll be acting

152

out Druid girl abducted by Briton,' he said, hugging her back.

'I hope not,' said a familiar voice behind Ursula. 'I saw your act, and the two of you were wonderful together.'

Ursula's heart forgot to beat. Was she dreaming?

Prasutus was as pale as parchment. He was looking over her shoulder.

'It's clear,' said the familiar voice, 'that the two of you are meant for each other.'

Ursula turned to see the most beautiful youth in Britannia.

It was Castor, one of the boys she loved.

And he had just seen her hugging Prasutus.

Chapter Thirty-Nine
VINUM

'Castor!' Ursula ran to greet the boy she loved. 'Did you find Raven?' she asked. 'Is he here?'

Before he could answer, the others were crowding around to greet him.

'Where have you been?' Fronto asked.

'How have you been?' Bouda's green eyes were bright.

'We've been looking for your Uncle Jonathan,' said Juba. 'I don't suppose you've come across him in your travels?'

Castor shook his head and was about to ask something when Bircha pointed.

'Look!' she cried. 'There's Lupus! He knew you when you were a baby!'

Suddenly everyone was quiet, watching to see how Castor and Lupus would react. For a moment the two of them stood looking at one another. Lupus was as tawny, taut and sinewy as a rawhide plait, and Castor looked like a young Apollo carved of ivory and ebony.

Then Lupus was embracing the youth and thumping his back with his fist. This made Castor laugh and then choke back a sob, the first time Ursula had ever seen him near tears.

Later, after a light supper of cheese and barley cakes around a campfire with the yew trees black behind them, Lupus brought out a small amphora of Roman wine and filled their cups.

Ursula didn't usually drink wine, but with Gartha on her left and Castor on her right she was so happy that she held out her empty cup for some, too.

'Oh, that's good.' Castor closed his eyes as he sipped. 'It reminds me of Ostia.'

'It's from vineyards near Ostia,' said Clio softly. 'Lupus has been saving it for a special occasion. It's one of the few things he can almost taste.'

The wine was too strong for Ursula so she tipped the rest of hers into Castor's cup.

'Thank you,' he said, with a smiling glance. He looked pale and tired, yet still impossibly handsome.

'Now that you've eaten,' said Juba, 'tell us how you got on? Did you find Raven?'

'Sadly not,' said Castor, staring into his wine.

'Then how did you find us?' asked Clio.

Castor smiled. 'It was thanks to Lupus,' he said.

Lupus leaned forward, his eyes glinting green in the firelight.

'I was in the capital town of the region where Raven grew up,' explained Castor, 'but had no luck finding him or his mother. I had been there about a week when I heard some soldiers talking about Lupus the Pantomime Dancer and how his troupe was on its way to Eboracum. I remembered my grandmother used to talk about a mute friend of my uncle Jonathan by that name. He had become a famous pantomime dancer. I thought perhaps you might have some information about my brother.'

He drained his wine cup and looked at Ursula. 'I didn't expect to find *you* travelling with Lupus as part of his show. But you and Prasutus make a delightful couple.'

Ursula nodded and felt her face go hot. She wanted to tell him that she and Prasutus were only pretending to be lovers. But somehow the words would not come; her tongue was as sluggish as when she had first bitten it.

Juba said, 'Our patroness Flavia told us to join Lupus. We're trying to find your Uncle Jonathan who has been seeking your brother for half his life.'

Lupus held up his wax tablet. NO CLUE AT ALL ABOUT POPO? I MEAN RAVEN?

'No.' Castor shook his head. 'I found the village where his mother had lived and worked as a weaver. They told me she left a few months ago. Some people think she might have gone north. But nothing about my brother.' He put his dark head in his pale hands. In the firelight, Ursula saw where he had bitten his thumbnails to the quick. 'How will we ever find him? This province is so vast and nobody knows who he is . . .'

Ursula's heart melted for Castor. She touched the little ivory Venus down the front of her tunic. Then she whispered a prayer and a vow.

The idea came to her a moment later.

'I know how to find Raven!' she cried. 'I know how to get everyone in Britannia to help us search for your brother!'

Meer sensed her excitement and ran up on to her shoulder. Gartha panted and thumped her tail. Loquax said, '*Find Jonathan!*'

Castor raised his head. 'Everyone in Britannia?'

'Well, maybe half of everyone in Britannia.'

'Tell us!' they said. Even Prasutus, sitting in the shadows just outside the firelight, looked up with interest.

'No. You tell me.' She leaned forward, feeling the encouraging warmth of the fire on her face. 'How can you instantly get a message to thousands of people in this province?'

'A carrier pigeon?' suggested Bouda.

Ursula shook her head. 'A carrier pigeon only goes to one location.'

Fronto's scale armour glinted in the firelight as he stepped closer; he was on sentry duty. 'What if someone sent a carrier pigeon to the governor's palace in Londinium?' he said. 'As we've done before?'

'Yes!' cried Clio, who was sitting beside Lupus on the other side of the fire. 'And the governor sends out a decree!'

'With lots of heralds on fast horses,' said Juba. 'Riding along the best Roman roads!'

'The cursus publicus!' cried Fronto. 'Next to a carrier pigeon, it's the fastest way of sending a message.'

Ursula shook her head. 'Even better than that. And much faster.'

'If you can think of something faster and better than an imperial decree then I would be amazed,' said Castor.

Ursula laughed. 'What about an audience of five thousand men and women,' she said, 'who will then return to the forts and villages around with their news?'

'The crowds in the amphitheatre!' cried Castor, tossing back his glossy hair.

'Yes! We're about to perform before a big crowd, correct?'

'Yes,' said Fronto. 'One of the biggest yet. There might be as many as ten thousand if you count legionaries, auxiliaries and Britons . . .'

'And what do people love most of all?'

'Blood and guts?' said Bolianus.

'Beast fights?' offered Polyphemus, who was sitting in the shadows by his animals.

'Honey cakes?' said Fronto.

'Prizes and coins?' said Bouda.

'No! Remember when we were living with the Belgae and the three of us wore hooded cloaks and we became famous among all the tribes around without even leaving the village?'

'Mysterious hooded demigods!' cried Vindex. 'People love mysterious hooded demigods most of all!'

Ursula rolled her eyes. 'Do you really mean to say you can't guess what people love most?'

Chapter Forty
FABULA

'I'll give you all one last chance to guess,' said Ursula. 'What do people love most?'

Across the fire, Lupus grunted and held up his wax tablet. On it he had written STORIES.

'Yes!' cried Ursula, pointing at him. 'People love a story! They love Lupus's pantomimes and our bard's songs and knowing what happened next. That's why they really like beast fights and gladiators. They're all stories.'

'I still don't understand how that helps us find Raven,' said Juba with a scowl.

'I know how!' cried Clio. 'Lupus can dance the story.'

'Yes!' Ursula looked at Lupus. 'Instead of a myth, you will tell the real story of identical twins separated in infancy, and how Castor is looking for a boy exactly like himself. Just like you told it the first night we met you. Then those ten thousand people will tell their friends and families and they'll pass it on and before we know it someone will tell us where Raven is.'

'But how will they know what Raven looks like?' asked Vindex. Before anyone could reply, he struck his forehead with the heel of his hand. 'Of course! What a blockhead I am!'

'What?' cried Polyphemus, who had moved closer to hear. 'How will they know?'

'Because of me,' said Castor, his eyes shining. 'My brother looks exactly like me. All I have to do is go out on to the sand at the end of Lupus's show and then ten thousand people will know what my brother looks like.'

He looked at Ursula. 'Thank you,' he said. 'You are not only brave but also brilliant and beautiful.' He leaned over and kissed her on the cheek, causing Meer to purr loudly and Gartha to wag her tail.

But Prasutus was frowning. 'You want to tell ten thousand people about Raven? What if he doesn't want to be found?'

Castor's smile faded, and Ursula shot Prasutus an angry look.

But on the other side of the fire, Lupus nodded and pointed at Prasutus to show his agreement.

Encouraged by this, Prasutus continued. 'The last time you saw your brother, he tried to kill you.'

Lupus, Clio and Polyphemus all stared, bug-eyed. 'Your brother tried to *kill* you?' whispered Clio.

Castor scowled. 'He didn't try to kill me for long. He was just shocked to find out he was Roman by birth.'

Prasutus nodded. 'So shocked that he ran away.'

The fire gave a soft *pop* in the silence that followed, and sent some sparks floating up into the dark blue sky.

Juba lifted his head. 'I think Prasutus is right,' he said. 'What if Raven doesn't want to be found? I think we should let Raven find Castor when he's ready.' He prodded the fire with a stick, making it burn brighter. 'Personally,' he added, 'I hate being told what to do. And I hate people meddling in my life, even if they think they know best.'

'Why wouldn't Raven want to find his brother?' asked Clio. 'Why did he want to kill him?'

'Because they grew up in such different worlds,' said Bircha.

Prasutus nodded and ran his hand through his dark red hair. 'Just think about it,' he said. 'One day a person who looks exactly like you appears. He says your mother is not your mother but a woman who stole you as baby, and that your father is not your father but evil. And that you belong to a hated race of men. Your whole world is . . .' He struggled to find a word, then took his beaker and turned it upside down over the fire. The dregs of diluted wine made the flames hiss and spark. 'It makes your soul like that,' he said, pointing at the sputtering fire.

They all stared at the flames for a moment, then Ursula said, 'But see how quickly the fire recovered and now burns brightly again? What if Raven's soul also recovered and he became used to the idea that he is Roman? And what if he now wants to know more?'

Everyone was quiet for a moment. Some nodded their heads, others shook theirs.

Prasutus hung his head. 'I ran away, too,' he said. 'Because my stepfather beat me. I never want to be found by him.'

Ursula stared at him. He always seemed so happy and confident; she never suspected he was running from something.

Juba gave a rueful smile. 'I suppose we are on the run, too.'

'But we're also seeking.' Ursula stroked Meer, who had come in from hunting. 'That's what we've been called to do. Flavia Gemina wants us to help Lupus find Jonathan ben Mordecai.'

'Who is also seeking Raven,' said Fronto.

'Jonathan might not want to be found either,' said Clio. 'After all, he's taken another name: Prometheus.'

There was a long pause in which Ursula could hear the river gurgling, the fire crackling and an owl hooting somewhere.

'I think we should ask the gods what to do,' said Juba at last. 'Everybody get out your gods and we'll ask them for a sign.'

He fished down the neck of his tunic and brought out his statuette. Ursula saw that the little wings on Mercury's helmet were burnished almost gold with constant handling. She started to reach for her Venus when Lupus grunted as if to say *No* and shook his head. He was writing something on his wax tablet.

They all waited and at last he gave it to Clio.

'I am the one dancing,' she read on Lupus's behalf. 'My God has just told me to simply tell the story and let Castor show himself. But to beware of mentioning a reward.'

'Fair enough,' said Castor, tossing his hair.

Lupus was still writing and Clio read it in her clear voice.

'Also,' she read, 'we will tell of the doctor named Prometheus who has been searching for Raven half his life. After all, that is our quest.'

Chapter Forty-One
SALTATIO

Everyone said it was the best story Lupus the Pantomime had ever danced, and Ursula agreed.

For their second show at Eboracum, ten thousand people were captivated by the true story of twins separated soon after birth and then reunited a dozen years later after one of them made the perilous journey to the edge of the Empire.

To the haunting sound of drum, flute and lyre, Clio sang while Lupus danced. He danced the storm at sea. He danced the robbery and beating of Castor in Londinium. Ursula did not mind that she and her brothers and Bouda were not mentioned; after all, they were wanted fugitives. Lupus and his troupe kept the story simple. They showed Castor wandering among savage blue-painted Britons until he and his twin finally came face-to-face in a mysterious grove. Lupus danced Raven's shocking reaction to the discovery that he had a twin. And how the twins were separated again after only a few brief moments together.

Finally, Lupus danced the story of a doctor called Prometheus who had been searching for the missing twin half his life.

The audience laughed. They cried. They gasped.

At the end, when Castor pushed past Ursula and the others to show himself in the arena, several women fainted at the sight of his youthful beauty, and the rest went silent with wonder. His eyes had been lined with black and his smooth cheeks touched with a hint of pink. His black hair, as straight and shiny as a raven's wing, skimmed his shoulders. Even Ursula felt dizzy.

'My brother,' cried Castor in a clear voice, 'looks exactly like me. He is my identical twin.'

Then, with a defiant glance at Lupus, he continued. 'We are on our way to the great colonia of Camulodunum to put on our final show for the people there. We expect to reach that town a week from tomorrow, seven days before the Kalends of August.' Castor took a breath and cried, 'I offer one thousand sesterces to any person who can produce my twin brother, alive and unharmed. Bring my twin to Camulodunum if you want the reward!'

Ursula gasped. 'He swore he wouldn't offer a reward!'

'That fool!' cried Juba beside her. 'Look what's happening!'

The great amphitheatre was buzzing like a bowl of bees. Several people were already making their way to the exits, although the main event had not yet started.

'Montanus is not happy,' Prasutus observed. 'And Vegetus's face is red.'

Ursula realised her mouth was open. Now Castor was moving across the sand towards them, his hair and cloak lifting a little with each stride. He had a strange smile on his face and his kohl-lined eyes were fixed on something beyond them all.

'Are you mad?' cried Vegetus, rushing after him. 'We'll be overwhelmed with reports of your brother.'

'No we won't,' said Castor as he moved from the bright arena into the dim holding cell. 'The only way they will get the reward is by bringing me Raven himself, unharmed.'

'But where will you find a thousand sesterces for the reward?' spluttered Vegetus.

'From Juba,' said Castor. 'He can sell one of his jewels.'

Juba stared open-mouthed in astonishment, too stunned to speak.

Castor waved airily. 'I'll give you my ship if necessary. But I have to find him. I *have* to!'

Ursula noticed that her cat was weaving around Castor's ankles and purring. As he started to move away, he half-tripped on her. With a muttered curse and a sideways kick of his foot, Castor sent Meer tumbling out from under the hem of his cloak.

'*Meeer!*'

It was only a small gesture of impatience but it made Ursula's heart twist. How could he kick Meer, who adored him?

She felt a strange heat rising up from her knees to her belly and then her heart. Everything suddenly looked unnaturally sharp, like the time she had become a bird. She seemed to taste the bitter potion she had drunk under the Druid moon.

'Ursula?' Prasutus was looking at her with eyes full of concern. They were dark blue, and kind.

She realised that she loved him. She loved Prasutus.

She loved him as much as she loved Raven and Castor.

And she loved Bircha and Bolianus and Bouda and her brothers and Vindex . . . And even red-faced Vegetus.

She realised she loved them all.

Ursula caught her breath as she felt a huge wave of love for everyone and everything around her. The emotion squeezed her like a sponge. She wanted to weep.

'She's about to have another seizure!' Prasutus's voice seemed to come from a great distance. 'Get a birch switch or a piece of leather to put between her teeth,' he cried. 'Anything!'

The wave of love lifted her high, and then drained utterly away.

Before the backwash of pain crashed her into unconsciousness, she had an exquisite moment of clarity.

I'm meant to be here, she thought. *I'm meant to be here in this time and this place, in the dim, animal-scented twilight beneath the seating of an amphitheatre.*

3

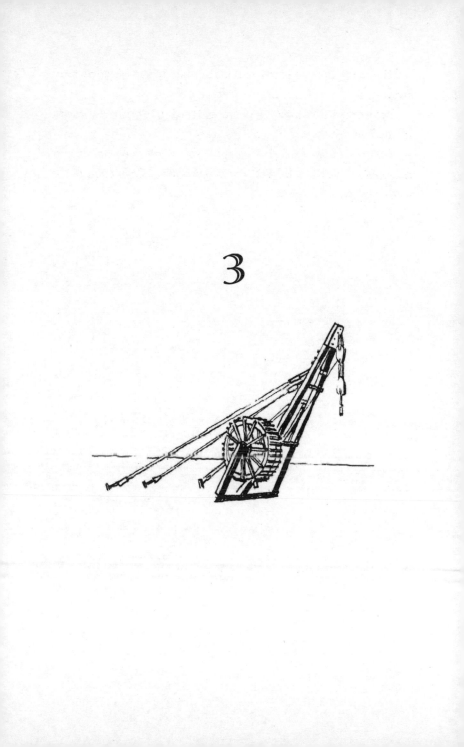

Chapter Forty-Two
FEBRIS

Ursula did not recover from this second seizure as quickly as she had the first time. This time, a fever made her skin as hot as a loaf fresh from the oven.

And, like a loaf, she was hot inside, too. Sometimes a moist cloth cooled her face and throat. Sometimes they gave her sips of water. The hands were so gentle that she thought it might be her mother. Then she remembered: her mother was dead.

She wanted to weep but had no tears.

Instead, she had dreams.

She dreamt of being in a place of sand and heat, like the deserts her father had told her about.

She dreamt she was inside a potter's kiln.

She even dreamt of flames that burned her but did not consume.

The clearest dream was of being a gladiatrix, a female gladiator. But she was on a racecourse not in an arena, and she was wearing her cormorant-feather cloak instead of armour. She stood alone on the sand. All around her, in the stands, were a million spectators. They were made of light, and they were cheering her on.

Then came her opponent.

He was a giant, twice as big as Polyphemus. He wore armour of black iron with a bird's-head helmet. It had a long beak and through the circular eyeholes, she could see his pupils glinting red.

Sometimes she heard people speaking outside her fever. She recognised the voices of her brothers, and also the voices of Bouda and Prasutus. Once she thought she heard the wheezing voice of Montanus, their important patron.

Sometimes she heard Meer's purr or Loquax telling visitors to '*Carpe diem!*', '*Ave, Domitian!*' or '*Find Jonathan!*' But most of all she felt a cool tongue on her cheek and smelled dog breath and heard soft whining.

'I've never seen Gartha like this,' came the voice of Polyphemus. 'She won't fight, she won't dance and she won't even eat.'

She could smell Gartha's doggy smell, and the vinegary whiff of posca, and the sweet scent of cool honeywater. She was always thirsty but although she drank buckets, she never seemed to need to pee.

Later, she was aware of being in the dim and noisy interior of the carruca, lying on one of the benches. She could feel the rocking, hear the change of tone as the wheels ground over stone or gravel or mud. Sometimes all was still and the world so quiet that she could hear distant music or cheering.

'Her body is too hot,' came a man's voice one day. 'The moisture leaves her body as sweat. She must be cooled all over. Preferably by running water. A stream is best, but the cold plunge of a bath will do. Then you must dry her off, wrap her in muslin and give her ptisan to drink, and white fish soup.'

'What is ptisan?' That was Bouda's voice.

'Barley water sweetened with honey. You can give her lettuce, too, if there is any to be found.'

The next thing Ursula knew, she was being carried in the arms of a giant. It was not the giant opponent of her dreams, but someone else. Her eyes were glued shut but she could smell lotus blossom and bear urine. Polyphemus was carrying her outside. She could hear birdsong and see dappled light on the red of her eyelids that still would not open. And now she was being lowered into cold running water: a brook or stream. The flowing water carried away the excess heat from her skin. It was deliciously cool and she wanted to stay there forever.

And then, suddenly, she was too cold. Her teeth were chattering and her body shaking. 'Take her out!' came the man's voice. 'Wrap her in sindon.'

'What is sindon?' Again: Bouda's voice.

'Muslin,' said the man. 'Fine linen.'

Presently she felt them wrapping her like a cocoon. The sindon was fresh and clean and soft, and it smelled of sunshine and the meadow. She knew it was the sweet nettle-cloth fabric that Bouda had been weaving for Fronto in the cool of the mornings. Soon, her shivering stopped. They made her sip warm fish soup and cool, honey-sweetened barley water.

She slept for a short time, but presently the furnace inside her made her feverish again, so they took her back to the stream.

They repeated this three times and then carried her to the carruca, for the day was getting cooler and the red behind her eyelids was brown. Night was coming.

She heard music being played, the distinctive sound of Lupus's troupe. She wondered if he was dancing a story. She wanted to tell him to stop and wait for her to wake up, but presently she drifted away.

Ursula slept for a long time, and woke needing to pee.

But she could not rise from her cot or even open her eyes; they seemed glued by sleep. With great effort, she managed to open them enough to see a blurred world of black and silver with the brown shapes of people moving in it, but she could not move her body or even tell where she was. Was she still in the carruca? Or an inn? She could not even remember where they had last been. She tried to fight her way out of the prison her body had become.

Once she had been a bird. Now she was a rock.

'She's awake! I think she's awake!'

It was Bouda's voice. Faithful Bouda, the British girl whom she had never fully trusted. Somehow, Ursula knew that Bouda had been with her almost the whole time. She tried to speak, tried to see, but everything was stuck together.

'Bathe her face in cool water,' came the now familiar man's voice. 'The fever has sealed her mouth and eyes.'

A soft sea-sponge with cool water bathed her face, and at last she was able to open her eyes.

She was still in the carruca. The back door was open and brilliant morning light showed Bouda with a sponge and behind her Juba, both looking concerned. Then another face loomed into view. It was a man's face, strange and yet familiar.

The man had kind brown eyes in a squarish face beneath curly dark hair. He was smiling. 'Welcome back to the land of the living,' he said in flawless Latin. She tried to remember where she had seen a face like his before.

Then it came to her: the portrait on the outside of Lupus's wax tablet.

That was where she had seen his face.

'Doctor Jonathan?' she croaked.

He smiled and nodded.

'How did we find you?' she managed to ask.

'You didn't find me,' he said. 'I found you.'

Chapter Forty-Three
CAMULODUNUM

Ursula was amazed to hear that she had been feverish for almost a week.

As Bouda and Bircha helped her sit up on her bed in the carruca, they told her how they had convinced Vegetus to wait an entire day at Eboracum, hoping her fever would pass. But Montanus himself had come and told them the show must continue its tour, so they had put her in the carriage and headed south. They told her about a terrifying ferry crossing at Petuaria and how Juba had tried – and failed – to take her place in the chariot act at a small fort called Lindum. In the end Lupus had to do it, wearing a wig and pretending to be an Amazon. They both laughed at the memory. Ursula smiled, too, and stroked Gartha's head.

Bouda told her that they were beginning to despair of her coming out of her fever, when a man on a mule arrived at their camp one evening.

It was Doctor Jonathan, who had heard the story of the separated twins and the doctor Prometheus and the reward to be given at Camulodunum.

'He and Lupus hugged each other for a long time,' said Bircha. 'And Lupus *cried*! Apparently they hadn't seen each other for over ten years!'

'But when we told Doctor Jonathan you had a fever he came straight to see you,' said Bouda. 'Gartha wouldn't let him near you at first,' she added.

At the mention of her name, Gartha whined softly and looked up at Ursula, her brown eyes full of devotion. Ursula gave the faithful hound a hug.

Bouda shook her head. 'What did you do to earn her love?' she asked. 'She was with you the whole time and hardly ate at all.'

'I didn't do anything,' said Ursula, scratching Gartha behind the ear. 'She must know how much I love her. Help me up?'

She sat up on the carruca bench and they came to support her.

'Where are we now?' She had to shade her eyes against bright sunlight as they helped her down from the carruca. It was about the second hour of a brilliant summer morning.

'We're somewhere on the outskirts of Camulodunum,' said Bircha.

'That was one of the three towns destroyed by my great-grandmother thirty-five years ago,' said Bouda, almost proudly.

'You'd better not tell them who you are.' Ursula laughed, then staggered and had to steady herself on Gartha, who was close beside her.

As her eyes adjusted to the brightness, she saw they had made camp beside a stream. Tunics and cloaks had been spread over bushes and were steaming in the morning sun. It must be a rest day: Bouda and Bircha had been washing clothes.

Juba left the campfire to give her a hug. 'I'm making you fish broth,' he said. 'Are you feeling better?'

She nodded and rested in his arms for a moment. It seemed he had grown over the past week.

Lupus emerged from bushes near the stream with three fine fish in a hand net. He beamed when he saw her, gestured at his precious folding chair and bowed to her, as if to say, *Help yourself!* Then he went to clean the fish by the fire.

The girls helped Ursula to Lupus's folding chair, for her legs were wobbly.

'Not too close to the fire!' said a man's voice. Ursula noticed Doctor Jonathan sitting cross-legged in the shade of a tree. He was grinding something in a small bronze mortar. 'Bring her over here,' he said, rising to his feet.

Bircha carried the chair while Bouda and Gartha supported Ursula. When they reached the shady place, she was about to sink into Lupus's folding chair when Doctor Jonathan sat in it.

'Stand in front of me,' he commanded, 'so I may examine you. It's much better with you standing before me like this. Stick out your tongue?' he said.

Ursula stuck out her tongue until he told her to close her mouth again. She felt dizzy, so held on to Gartha's collar while Doctor Jonathan felt her neck, belly and legs. His fingers seemed to be reading her, like a blind man's. But they didn't just brush her, they sometimes poked and prodded. Presently he pressed the first three fingers of his right hand against the inside of her left wrist. She could feel her heart beating there.

He frowned. 'Have you been more than usually sensitive to light recently?'

She pondered this, then nodded. 'Ever since I went in an animal trance.'

'Animal trance?' He looked up sharply.

'I took a potion of mushroom, mistletoe and mugwort.'

'Mushrooms are tricky and mistletoe is poisonous,' he said. 'Every time you take it you're doing yourself harm. That potion

176

is certainly the cause of your seizures.' He let go of her wrist and stood up. 'I urge you to repent.'

'*Repent!*' said Loquax, settling on her right shoulder.

'What?'

Doctor Jonathan nodded. 'What the bird said. You know magic is illegal. Repent of your sinfulness and invite God's spirit to live within you. He will give you more wisdom and insight than any animal spirit.'

Ursula took a step backwards: she felt dizzy.

Gartha sensed her unease and growled at Jonathan.

Ursula patted Gartha to calm her. 'I don't want anybody's spirit living inside me,' she said, as Meer leapt up on to her shoulder. 'I only want me inside me.'

'Too late for that,' he said. 'You have several spirits already.'

Ursula laughed. 'Gartha, Meer and Loquax are my friends, not spirits.'

'No. Inside you. You have spirits inside you. Some call them demons.'

She looked at him in horror. 'Can you get them out?'

'No point. If I cast them out then others will take their place.' He closed his eyes and pinched the bridge of his nose. 'I once saw five demons cast out of a man. Each spoke with a different voice as it left. I begged him to invite in God's spirit but he refused. The next day he was hosting five hundred.'

Ursula shuddered. 'How many do I have now?' she asked in a small voice.

Jonathan sighed deeply and stood up. He gestured to the chair. 'Sit.'

Ursula sat. Loquax flew up but Meer remained, and Gartha curled up at her feet. Doctor Jonathan put his right hand on her head and she felt a heat, like the time Lupus had touched her.

She was about to ask again how many spirits were inside her when she saw that his eyes were closed. A slight frown brought his dark eyebrows together. Then his forehead grew smooth and he opened his eyes. 'I believe you have three spirits in you,' he said. 'The spirits of mouse, cat and bird.'

Ursula stared at him. How could he know about the three beasts she had entered at Mistletoe Grove?

'Did the others tell you what happened last month?' she asked him.

'Only that you drank some potion which included mistletoe. And that you were dabbling in sorcery. Both very dangerous things to do.'

'Are the spirits dangerous?' she asked in a small voice.

'Of course. They are not from the light, but from the dark. We must each battle our own animal natures. It doesn't help to add other animal spirits.'

'Can you get them out?'

'Only if you agree to invite in the Spirit of God.'

'Why do I have to do that?'

'So his spirit can dwell inside you, and stop other spirits coming in. Like a strong man who stops thieves entering his house.'

Ursula pondered this.

'He won't make you do things against your will,' said Jonathan. 'My God never forces you, only prompts. And he is always kind, gentle and just.'

Gartha raised her head and whined softly. 'Does he like animals?' asked Ursula, rubbing Gartha behind her ear.

Jonathan smiled. 'Very much. He knows when every sparrow falls to the ground. Also, his death means no more animal sacrifice. Ever.'

'Really? No more animal sacrifice?' Ursula stopped stroking Gartha's big head and looked at him in wonder.

He nodded. 'That was the argument that clinched it for my friend Nubia,' he added.

'She is a Christian, too?' asked Ursula. 'But not Flavia Gemina?'

Jonathan gave a rueful smile. 'Not yet. She's still deciding.'

Ursula touched the little ivory Venus down the front of her tunic. 'I'm still deciding, too. May I think about it?'

'Of course. But seriously consider repenting of your sin,' he said. 'It's like cleaning your house before the strongman comes in.'

Ursula frowned. 'What is sin? It sounds like something bad.'

'Sin is anything you do that you know is wrong. Especially anything you do for your own benefit and not for others.' Jonathan slowly reached over to stroke Gartha, who allowed it.

'And what is repent?'

'Repentance merely means to stop doing wrong things and start doing the right things.'

'But I didn't do the potion and magic for myself,' she protested. 'I did it to find Castor and Raven!'

Jonathan shook his head. 'The heart is deceitful above all things,' he murmured.

'Doctor Jonathan,' she said suddenly. 'What is the information you have that could bring down Emperor Domitian?'

He looked at her for a long moment, his dark eyes very grave. 'His most trusted astrologer told me the day and even the hour of his death.'

'And you believe him?'

'It's not important that I believe him,' replied the doctor. 'What's important is that Domitian believes him.'

179

Before Ursula could ask when this fated day would come, the clattering of hoofbeats on the road made them all look up.

It was Prasutus driving the white team, his face pale and eyes wide.

'Terrible news!' He jumped off the chariot while it was still moving. 'I've just been into Camulodunum with Castor. Someone found Raven. He's in the city!'

'But that's good news, surely?' said Juba, still holding the wooden spoon from stirring the broth.

'No.' Prasutus's chest was rising and falling, as if he had been running and not driving a chariot. 'Someone has denounced them and they've both been arrested!'

'Arrested?' cried Ursula.

'Under what charge?' Juba asked.

'Raven is accused of being a Druid and Castor of being a Jew. They're going on trial in less than an hour. If nobody defends them they will be executed as criminals in the arena tomorrow!'

Chapter Forty-Four
DIVINATIO

'Raven and Castor might be condemned to the beasts?' Ursula stood up so suddenly that world seemed to tip and she had to sit down again.

'You must be mistaken,' she heard Doctor Jonathan say. 'It's not a crime to be a Jew. Domitian imposed a special tax on us, but our religion is not illegal.'

'He's right,' said Juba. 'I know because lots of my father's best gem suppliers were Jews.'

'But aren't Jews the same as Christians?' Bircha asked.

Jonathan shook his head. 'A few Jews, like me, are Christians, and that's why the rest hate them.'

'You're a Christian?' Juba's grey-green eyes were wide.

Doctor Jonathan shrugged and then gave a rueful nod.

'Wait!' cried Bouda. 'Can't the twins just promise to worship Domitian and to obey Roman laws? Then they can go free. Like that skinny Jew did last week.'

'That is not the charge,' said Prasutus. 'They are accused of divination.'

'Why divination?' said Juba and Bouda together.

'They found forbidden objects on them. Castor had a scroll

with magic marks. And Raven had a golden sickle on a cord round his neck.'

Jonathan shook his head. 'The magic marks were probably just Hebrew letters,' he said. 'It is a different alphabet from Latin or Greek.'

'Doctor Jonathan!' cried Ursula. 'You have to help them!'

Lupus nodded and held up his wax tablet. PLEAD THEIR CASE?

'Can anybody plead a case?' asked Bouda. 'Don't you have to be trained?'

'You have to be a Roman citizen,' said Juba, 'and at least fifteen. That is, wearing the toga virilis. Otherwise I would do it myself.' He turned to Doctor Jonathan. 'Are you a Roman citizen?'

They all looked hopefully at the doctor.

He hesitated. 'Yes, but I've never argued a case in court before.'

YOU'VE SEEN IT DONE! wrote Lupus.

Jonathan ben Mordecai stared at his hands. 'If I plead his case, I'll have to give my real name.'

'Is that a problem?' asked Juba.

Jonathan nodded. 'There's an imperial warrant out for my arrest.'

Juba gave a bitter laugh. 'Join the guild.' He gestured around at the others.

Fronto clanked as he stepped forward, his face grave. 'But *we* won't be giving our names out in a public court of law.'

There was a long moment of silence, then Ursula took the doctor's hands in hers. 'Please, Doctor Jonathan?'

Lupus held up his tablet, his expression almost regretful. On it he had written, SOSO AND POPO. MIRIAM'S TWINS.

Jonathan sighed. 'Of course I must go! I've spent the past twelve years longing to reunite the twins. How can I not try to help them?' He reached for his nutmeg-brown cloak and fastened it with a fibula.

'Shouldn't you be wearing a toga?' asked Juba.

Jonathan looked around their riverside camp as if trying to remember where he was. 'I'm not sure what they do here in the provinces,' he said.

Lupus held up a finger, then ran to the pantomime wagon. A moment later he was back with a folded toga. Ursula caught a whiff of something that made her think of home. The toga had been sprinkled with drops of camphor to keep away moths, just as her father had always done.

'Good idea.' Doctor Jonathan started to unfold the toga, which was as big as a blanket. 'But I'm not sure I can put it on. Most men who wear these have slaves to help them.'

'I think I can help,' said Juba. 'I watched the slaves dress my father sometimes. I'll take you in the chariot,' he added. 'By the sound of it, we don't have a moment to lose.'

'Let me come with you!' cried Ursula. But she got up too suddenly and the world tilted again.

'Whoa!' said Prasutus, steadying her with his hands. 'You've only just got up from your sick bed. You should rest.'

'No!' she cried, moving out of his grasp. 'I want to go.'

'Come on, Ursula.' Bouda's tone was patient. 'There's nothing you can do. Let me take you back to the carruca.'

'No! I don't want to go back to bed!' Ursula fought back tears of frustration. 'I've been in bed for a week. I want to help Castor and Raven!'

Sensing her anger, Gartha growled at Bouda.

Bouda stood back, astonished. For a moment her green eyes

183

were wide, then she narrowed them at Ursula. 'Go and lie down, before one of us says something we can never take back.'

'No!' Ursula pushed Bouda away. 'How can you be so calm? I know you love Castor!'

They all stared at Bouda.

Juba was the first to speak. 'You love Castor?'

'Don't worry,' Ursula said to Bouda. 'I've decided you can have Castor and I'll marry Raven.'

They were all staring at her with open mouths, so she quickly added, 'If they want to, of course.'

'And if I win my case,' muttered Jonathan, 'and they aren't executed.'

Bouda was shaking her head in disbelief. 'Come back to the carruca before you utter any more wool fluff.' She gently took Ursula's arm.

'It's not wool fluff!' Ursula threw off Bouda's supporting arm. 'I know you secretly love Castor. When we were at the sacred hot springs last year you put in a whole denarius and asked the goddess to make him love you!'

Bouda stood staring at Ursula, her mouth open. She looked as if someone had emptied a bucket of water on her head. Then she narrowed her eyes. 'You are completely wrong, you meddling child! You've ruined their lives, but I won't have you ruining mine!'

Ursula frowned. 'What do you mean? Whose lives have I ruined?'

'Bouda, stop!' cried Juba. 'You've said enough!'

Bouda ignored him. 'If you hadn't made Lupus perform Castor's story, they wouldn't have been summoned to court.'

'No more, Bouda! Please!' Juba put his hand on her shoulder but she batted it away and kept her eyes fixed on Ursula.

'It's *your* fault the twins have been arrested,' continued Bouda. 'And if they are tortured or executed that will be your fault, too.'

Ursula stared at Bouda. Her green eyes were blazing and her copper-coloured hair seemed to send off sparks in the morning sunshine.

The British girl was furious.

And Ursula knew she had every right to be so.

It was completely her fault that Castor and his brother had been sentenced to death in the arena.

Chapter Forty-Five
BASILICA

With Fronto and Vindex trotting ahead, Juba followed in the chariot, driving as fast as he dared. Doctor Jonathan sat on the leather-webbing floor, facing backwards and grimly hanging on to two of the four side arches of the light vehicle. The folded toga lay in his lap.

'I hate riding fast in chariots,' came the doctor's voice behind him. 'They make me feel sick.'

Juba nodded, but instead of slowing down he flicked the reins. He had to keep up with Fronto and Vindex, whose glittering fish-scale backs and plumed helmets were almost out of sight.

The river ran on their left, sometimes hidden by lush willows and sometimes glinting in the sunlight. A softly clanking flock of sheep scattered as they approached the town wall, and so did a flock of naked children who had been bathing in the river. Up above, the blue sky was marked with faint high clouds in a herringbone pattern. It seemed too perfect a morning for a tragedy to occur.

They entered the town through the north gate and found the basilica opposite the theatre. Vindex stayed outside to guard the chariot and horses while Fronto parted the crowds to guide

186

them through. Juba had hurriedly draped the toga around the doctor. It did not look quite right – part of it dragged on the ground behind him – but it would have to do.

When they entered the vast space of the basilica they saw the empty judge's chair on a marble podium above the heads of a crowd.

'Are we too late for the trial of the twins?' Doctor Jonathan asked a man in a toga.

'No,' he replied. 'They've just brought the prisoners in.'

Fronto led the way through the crowd. 'Defence lawyer coming through,' he cried, banging the butt of his javelin on the marble floor. 'Make way!'

The twins stood a few paces apart at the foot of the judge's raised platform. Both had their wrists tied behind and a soldier beside them. Both wore grubby tunics, but Raven also had leggings. Castor was looking at Raven, who stared angrily ahead.

'Master of the universe!' murmured Jonathan. 'They look so much like their mother.'

'Raven looks angry with Castor,' said Juba to the doctor.

'Can you blame him?' said Doctor Jonathan. 'From what you've told me, his brother virtually had him arrested and brought here to his death.'

One of the officials said something to Castor. He turned his head and relief flooded his face. 'Uncle Jonathan!' he called out. 'Can you help us? No one is willing to defend us!'

'That's why I'm here.' Doctor Jonathan stopped in front of Raven, who was still glaring straight ahead.

The crowd sensed a moment and grew silent. Even Raven turned his eyes to look at him.

'I am your uncle,' said Jonathan, his voice hoarse with

emotion. 'I've been seeking you for thirteen years. And now I'm here to defend you.'

For a moment, something flickered in Raven's eyes. Then his face grew hard again and he looked away.

'Don't mind him,' Castor whispered in Doctor Jonathan's ear. 'He's confused and scared.' Castor hung his head. 'Like me.'

'Me, too.' Doctor Jonathan patted his shoulder. 'Pray that God grants me favour.'

The herald mounted the marble dais and thumped his staff on the floor, even though the crowd was still silent. 'Usually the governor would judge such a case!' he cried. 'But he is not here and today we have someone just as important, the representative of our lord and god, the Emperor Domitian.'

'Montanus!' Doctor Jonathan's face had gone almost as white as the toga Juba was adjusting.

Juba turned to see the fat editor of the games puffing up the stairs of the podium. 'That's not fair!' he hissed. Then he stared at Doctor Jonathan. 'Wait! You know him?'

Jonathan nodded grimly as Montanus sank into the judge's chair. 'I saw him once fourteen years ago. He's one of Domitian's entourage. Some called him Helluo, the glutton.'

Juba swallowed hard. 'I guess we forgot to tell you he's the editor of the games.'

'Senator Gaius Curtius Montanus will be our judge!' blared the herald.

'What are the charges against these two boys?' wheezed Montanus. 'And who brings them?'

The crowd parted to reveal a man in a leek-green tunic. 'I do!' said the man. 'The charge is practising magic.'

'Vegetus!' Juba turned to Jonathan and whispered in his ear. 'This is some kind of plot. Montanus desperately needs a good event for their final show, in order to please the Emperor. There's no way you can win this case.'

'Thank you for those encouraging words,' muttered Doctor Jonathan.

'Speaking for the defence is Jonathan ben Mordecai,' blared the herald. 'A doctor from Ephesus.'

Jonathan was watching Montanus for a reaction. He closed his eyes with relief as he saw no sign that the fat man had recognised either his face or his name.

Next, the herald introduced the four lawyers for the prosecution. All four spoke first. They pleaded at great length with gestures and flourishes. Ultimately, all four said the same thing: the evidence of magic letters and a Druid sickle was proof of their crime.

Finally it was Doctor Jonathan's turn. With the toga draped awkwardly around him, he argued for mercy. He spoke eloquently about the terrible past of the twins and the anguish both had suffered. He said that the scroll of magic incantations was merely a commentary on some of the holy writings of the Jews. He said that the golden sickle was a trophy taken from a dead enemy, rather than an implement of infernal magic.

It did not take Montanus long to decide.

The herald banged his bronze-tipped staff for attention and Montanus rose to his feet.

'I find myself only partly convinced,' he wheezed. 'I decree that they will *not* be torn by beasts until dead.'

Half the spectators cheered and half booed.

'However,' Montanus raised his hand for silence, 'the practice of sorcery is both dangerous and illegal. It must not go unpunished. I therefore sentence them to battle one another to the death at tomorrow's games.'

Several women screamed and one fainted, but most people cheered.

'That means,' said Montanus, 'that at least one of them must die. Justice will not be mocked. Take them to the prison,' he wheezed to the guards. 'Separate cells!'

'Dear Jupiter,' whispered Juba. 'That means that one of them has to kill the other. That's worse than killing them both.'

'I should have known,' said Doctor Jonathan to Juba as they drove slowly back to their camp. 'I spend half my life looking for someone, and the day I find him he is sentenced to either death or a lifetime of guilt.'

Chapter Forty-Six
SCAENA

Fronto had seen small amphitheatres and vast ones, wooden and stone, half-empty and full to overflowing. But he had never seen the games performed in a theatre. This one only held about three thousand people, a quarter of the capacity of the biggest amphitheatre in Britannia.

It was the day of the games at Camulodunum and Montanus had asked him and Vindex to stand guard in the smaller than usual space, for there were rumours of riots.

The sacrifice was more vivid than any he had witnessed before. The marble backdrop threw back the single bleat of the dying ram and even the sound of its blood gushing into the silver bowl.

There were some mutterings over the omens, but after a longer than usual pause, Vegetus went up to the stage and announced a morning of entertainment sponsored by the great Emperor Domitian.

As always, the name sent a shiver through Fronto and he discreetly used his forefinger to tap his javelin for luck: *right, left, right.*

'Have you seen the changes to the programme?' he heard someone on his left say in Latin. A sideways glance told Fronto that the grey-haired man who had spoken was probably a veteran.

A bald man next to him nodded. 'Apparently there's a big crowd outside hoping to get in.'

'They should have held these games at the hippodrome,' observed Veteran One.

'They've only just started building it,' said Veteran Two.

'Better than a riot,' said Veteran One.

'No barriers against beasts,' said Veteran Three.

'They should have the beast fight here and then hold the gladiatorial combats and executions over there. That way everyone could come.'

'Shhh! Here comes the bear!'

A quarter of an hour later, the theatre was full of applause as Gartha and Big Ursula danced. Fronto tried not to grin. His younger sister's idea of finishing the animal combat this way had proved a great success. He noticed the veterans at the end of the row wiping tears from their leathery cheeks. He wondered if they would be as soft-hearted when the twins fought each other to the death.

When Lupus appeared to dance the story of how the warrior Achilles killed a fierce Amazon queen, Fronto stood a little taller, for Bircha and Bolianus were playing the instruments. Clio's voice had never sounded so pure or strong. Lupus made the audience gasp, cheer and cry. But Fronto could not take his eyes off Bircha, whose pink stola matched the flowers in her garland.

Once, in a quiet moment when she was not playing her flute, Bircha caught his eye and gave him a sad smile.

Fronto felt his cheeks go warm. For almost a year he had thought he loved red-haired Bouda, but her nature was too quick and slippery for him. He never knew what she was thinking. Bircha was almost transparent in her thoughts, and beautiful in body and soul.

Fronto forced himself to scan the crowd for the beginnings of a riot, but his eyes kept returning to the stage.

In the intimate space of the theatre, he could see each gesture Lupus made and even the movement of his eyes behind the mask. It amazed him how the combination of movement and eyes could make the blank mask express anger, surprise and grief.

It occurred to Fronto that a theatre like this was really the best place to hold a show.

But he was wrong. The space was too small to hold all the people who wanted to watch the famous pantomime dancer and the battle of Castor and his twin brother Raven. Lupus and his troupe were still taking their bows when the side doors of the theatre were broken down and the crowds rushed in.

It was everything he and the other soldiers could do to hold back the crowds long enough to let Lupus, Bircha and the others get to safety.

Chapter Forty-Seven
CIRCUS

When Doctor Jonathan arrived back at their camp beside the river with a clatter of hooves, Ursula looked up from her ivory figurine of Venus with tear-swollen eyes. 'Is it over?' she cried. She had been praying as hard as she could and making all sorts of vows, but had felt no sense of reassurance from the goddess. 'Are they dead?'

Jonathan shook his head as he dismounted. 'You're more of a pessimist than I am,' he said, and then, 'Nobody's dead yet. They were holding the games in the theatre but lots of people couldn't get in, me included. They're going to resume the executions and gladiatorial combats in the racecourse in two hours, an hour past midday.' He looked around. 'Are any of the others back yet?'

She shook her head. The word 'racecourse' reminded her of something. Something important.

Doctor Jonathan frowned. 'Some impulse told me to come back here. I can't think why . . .'

Ursula gasped. 'Doctor Jonathan, you have to take me there!'

'Absolutely not. You're too weak.'

'But I'm meant to be there! When I was in the fever, I had a dream. I was a gladiatrix fighting a man in a black bird mask. A raven!' She grabbed his arm. 'And I remember thinking it

194

strange that we were on a racetrack, not in an arena. Also, I was wearing my cormorant-feather cloak.'

He frowned. 'Dreams can be prophetic.'

'We have to go to the racecourse! You've got to take me!'

Ursula was expecting him to refuse again, and was surprised when he nodded.

'Yes,' he said. 'That must have been why the Lord prompted me to come back here.' He began to unhitch the ponies from the chariot.

'Aren't we taking the chariot? It's small and fast.'

'Not small enough; the roads are packed. We'll go faster on foot.'

Ursula ran to get her cormorant-feather cloak and also her cat and talking bird. Soon they were walking along a path beside the town wall ditch. Once around the south side of the town walls they could see a huge wooden crane rising up above trees and tombs to the southwest.

'See the polyspaston?' Doctor Jonathan lifted his chin towards the crane. 'That must be the new racecourse.'

'*Polyspaston!*' echoed Loquax.

It was not far, but it took them another half hour to make their way through the crowds to the hippodrome. Blocks of greenish sandstone the size of Big Ursula's cage stood stacked and ready. One of these stones was curved on top.

'*The stone the builders rejected has become the capstone,*' murmured Doctor Jonathan. Ursula could tell from his voice that he was quoting someone.

'What's a capstone?' she asked. On her shoulder, Meer was trying to keep her balance on the slippery feathers.

He pointed. 'The capstone is the final stone of the arch. It looks different from the rest because it has to fit in that wedge

195

space. Its weight holds all the other stones in place, which is why it's the most important.' He pointed to the crane. 'That polyspaston will soon lower it in place.'

Men, women and children were making their way to the curved end of the racecourse. Most passed through the unfinished arch, but some had found another way up a steep bank of earth. Meer clung tightly as Ursula started up this and the doctor followed, muttering under his breath.

As she topped the rise she could see the racecourse stretched out for the first time.

It looked like two long ribbons of earth with a narrow brick reservoir dividing them. She knew the brick part was called the euripus. When the racecourse was finished, it would be filled with water to be sprinkled on the track to keep down the dust. But now it was empty, for the hippodrome was not yet finished.

The long track was mainly mud, except at this end, where slaves were spreading fresh sand.

There were some wooden benches on the south side, but they were mostly taken by soldiers and Romans.

Here on the north bank, Ursula could see many local Britons. They seemed cheerful, carrying food in baskets and beer in leather skins. They sat on the earth bank, spreading their cloaks first, and pulled out bread, cheese and fruit.

A rank of solders marched on to the freshly sanded curve of the racecourse. Under the barking commands of their centurion they split into two groups, spread out on both sides of the track, and stood to attention facing the unfinished arch.

'What are they doing?' asked Ursula.

'Making a wall,' said Doctor Jonathan. 'With interlocked shields and their spears poking out, they can hold off most creatures.'

A blare of trumpets was followed by a commotion in the wooden stands, as the most important citizens of Camulodunum made way for Montanus. Two slaves placed a folding chair in front of the benches and the fat man took his seat.

'That's Montanus,' whispered Ursula. 'Sent by the Emperor.'

'I know.' Doctor Jonathan's grim tone of voice made her look sharply at him.

'You've met him before?'

'Several times, including yesterday morning at the basilica. He was the judge who sentenced the twins to mortal combat. Thankfully he didn't recognise me.'

Another blast from the horns commanded silence. 'That man in green is Vegetus,' said Ursula. 'But where are the twins? I don't see them anywhere.' She clutched his arm as a tiny bubble of hope rose in her heart. 'Doctor Jonathan, maybe he's not going to make them fight after all!'

Chapter Forty-Eight
SACRIFICIUM

Ursula watched Vegetus stop halfway between a huge cone of pale pink marble and the unfinished arch.

'The omens this morning were not propitious,' announced the fat man, 'and we nearly had a riot when people could not get in to see.' He gestured down to the makeshift arena. 'We will therefore sacrifice another ram to the genius of our Emperor and distribute meat from both at the end of these games.'

A cheer rose up, but Ursula's heart melted as a young ram followed two bare-chested helpers towards the priest who waited by a laurel-burning brazier.

Ursula stroked Meer to comfort her. Then she looked at Doctor Jonathan. 'Remember when you told me about the sparrows and no more sacrifice ever?'

Jonathan nodded. 'It's true,' he said. 'No more animal sacrifice for those who follow His Way.'

'Why?'

'Because Jesus was the final sacrifice, once and for all. He gave his life to save ours.'

'Did you hear that, Meer?' Ursula kissed the top of her big kitten's head. 'No more sacrifice.'

The priest must have trained the ram, for when he asked if it would submit to die, the creature bowed his garlanded head and went down on one knee. Ursula's eyes filled with tears as the axe fell, the knife cut and the blood flowed. She couldn't hear what the priest said, but the omens must have been favourable, for he nodded to fat Montanus up in the stands.

As the priest departed and his helpers removed the dead ram and the brazier trailing laurel-scented smoke, Vegetus addressed the crowds.

'For the past three weeks,' he blared, 'we have been touring forts and fortresses with our show. It is a gift to all of you who dwell in this province so dear to our Princeps, the divine Domitian.'

The crowds cheered happily.

'We have given you beast fights!'

The cheers were only moderate.

'Gladiator combats!'

The cheers were more robust.

'Lupus Pantomimus and his troupe!'

The cheers were enthusiastic.

'And the execution of criminals!'

The cheers were rapturous.

'And so, for the final execution of this tour, we present two beautiful youths, identical twins raised on different sides of the world.'

Ursula's heart sank as she heard these words.

'Only recently reunited,' blared Vegetus, 'they have both been accused of practising magic! Yesterday the court decreed that one be spared and one die. And now, in accordance with that decree, they will fight one another!'

The mixture of cheers, jeers and screams was almost deafening, and for a terrible moment the sky grew dark. Ursula thought she might faint. In desperation, she clutched the Venus down the front of her tunic and prayed, 'Venus, if you save the twins I vow to give you . . .' But she could not think what to vow.

'Doctor Jonathan?'

He was very pale, his eyes closed and his lips moving.

'Doctor Jonathan!' She shook his arm.

He opened his eyes. 'Yes?'

'How powerful is your God?'

'He is omnipotent.'

'What?'

'All-powerful. He can do anything. He created the whole universe. He sent his son Jesus and brought him back from the dead.'

'What do you call him?'

'What do you mean?'

'When you pray to your God, what do you call him?'

'You call him Lord.'

'Dear Lord.' Ursula closed her eyes and prayed out loud. 'Please stop this! Please throw a thunderbolt or swoop down in the form of an eagle.' She opened her eyes and looked up into the sky.

Beside her, Jonathan gave a sad smile. 'I'm afraid he doesn't work like that. He asks those of us who have accepted his sacrifice to be his hands and feet.'

'Then why don't *you* do something?'

He sighed. 'Yesterday I did my best and only succeeded in getting the judge to rule that one of them must kill the other.' He shook his head. 'Which is probably worse than the original sentence. One must die and the other must live with the guilt of killing his own brother for the rest of his life.'

All this time Ursula had been stroking Meer, but now she

200

stroked too hard and her cat meowed in protest and jumped on to the grass.

'Oh Doctor Jonathan!' She clutched his arm. 'I don't think I can bear it!'

Chapter Forty-Nine
SPECTACULUM

Overwhelmed by a sense of helplessness, Ursula hid her face in the crook of Doctor Jonathan's shoulder. He put his arm round her and patted her back as her father used to do.

'When I was not much older than you are now,' he said, 'I was almost executed in the arena.'

She pulled back and stared at him. 'Really?'

He nodded. 'The opening games of the Flavian amphitheatre in Rome. I fought as a secutor. But then I confessed to a crime. They tied me to a post and set a lion on me.'

Ursula gasped. 'What happened?'

'I prayed,' he replied. 'And help came from the most amazing place.'

'Oh! Was that when Nubia came down from the sky?'

'How do you know about that?'

'She and Flavia Gemina told us the story last year. Did Nubia save you?'

'No, she saved Flavia.' He cocked his head. 'You know, you remind me a little of them.'

'Of who?'

'Nubia and Flavia. You have Nubia's love for animals and Flavia's impulsiveness. And you're brave like both of them.'

Before Ursula could reply, horns blasted the audience into silence.

A collective gasp came from the crowd as half a dozen soldiers marched two hooded figures out on to the sand. One was wearing a black cloak, the other white. The soldiers stepped back and two beautiful girls in long tunics and flowered garlands stepped forward. One had straight pale blonde hair, the other a cloud of copper.

'Bircha and Bouda!' gasped Ursula. 'How could they?'

Then she gasped again as the girls removed the cloaks from the two figures.

Castor and Raven stood barefoot and naked apart from loincloths, one black, one white.

They were so beautiful that the breath was squeezed from her chest, and she felt dizzy. Nearby, a stocky mother with tawny hair lay down abruptly. Ursula realised the woman had fainted.

The twins stood facing each other, breathing hard, as if they had been running. Their bodies were lean and as pale as ivory, their straight black hair exactly the same length.

'Which one is Raven?' Jonathan asked.

'He's the one wearing black for raven . . . Unless he's wearing white for Druid. I don't know. I can't tell from up here.' Her throat was suddenly dry. 'Do you have anything to drink?'

He passed her his waterskin and she sucked greedily. It was ptisan, sweetened with honey and ginger. It gave her courage.

She looked around desperately for a way she could help the twins.

Then she saw the crane, leaning over the makeshift arena and the boys she loved standing below.

'Dear Lord God of Jonathan,' she prayed. 'Come live inside me, and help me save Castor and Raven.'

Jonathan was staring at her with wide brown eyes, and for a moment she could imagine him as a boy, not a tired doctor.

Ursula put Meer into his lap and stood up. 'Look after Meer?' She started to go but he caught her wrist.

'Before I let you go,' he said, 'tell me where you're going.'

Ursula pulled her hand free and gave him her bravest smile. 'I'm going to fly to their rescue.'

Chapter Fifty
POLYSPASTON

Ursula's cormorant-feather cloak fluttered behind her as she ran towards the massive wooden crane. It stood in a roped-off part of the seating and reminded Ursula of a sleeping giant. A skinny, sleeping giant leaning stiffly forward with his hands to his sides and with a cloak of ropes stretched out behind him so he would not topple on to his face. This 'crane-man' was made of several massive beams of wood, as tall as three lofty elms. His stomach was a wooden wheel close to the ground. Ursula knew that slaves or soldiers could walk inside that wheel. As it turned, the rope attached to the giant's chin would become taut and lift even the heaviest block hooked to its end.

However, the crane was not at work, so the hook of the rope was tied back to the crane's leaning body, about halfway down. The crane must have just lowered the pink cone-shaped block of marble that formed the meta, one of the two turning posts of the racecourse. That was why it was leaning out over the end of the circus.

Ursula knew that if she could get up to the hook and untie it, she could swing forward over the curved end of the hippodrome and save the twins.

But how to get up there?

She couldn't climb the ropes that anchored the crane in place. They were far too long and far too slippery.

She couldn't go up the wheel; it would just revolve under her weight.

The only way was to run up the beam of the crane itself. That beam stood at an angle that was halfway between standing up and lying down. If she lost momentum she would not make it.

But she didn't need to make it all the way up. She only needed to get as far as the big iron hook tied to the beam.

There were some boys standing near the crane. From here you could just see down into the racecourse. Even as she watched, one of them tried to climb the beam to get a better look, but he went too slowly and had to jump down on to the muddy earth underneath.

His friends laughed as they slapped the mud from his back.

Ursula reached into the neck of her tunic. 'Dear Venus,' she said. 'You have served me well and I will always remember you. Please forgive me for what I am about to do and do not be angry.'

The boys looked up at her as she came closer.

'Do any of you have a sharp knife?' she asked in good Brittonic.

They looked at each other. Then one of them, the boy who had fallen, pulled a small wooden-handled knife from a sheath on his belt.

Ursula nodded and held out her Venus. 'This is the Roman goddess Venus, the goddess of love. Not only will she grant you luck in love, but she is valuable. She is made of rare elephant tooth from a land so far you cannot imagine.'

'Africa,' said one of the other boys. His skin was brown like hers. 'My father is from the province of Mauretania,' he said, and to his friends, 'That's ivory. Worth a fortune.'

Ursula looked at the boy with the knife. 'I will trade my Venus for your knife and belt,' she said.

For a moment they were silent. Then they all clamoured to make the trade instead. They took off their belts or showed her their knives, bigger and better than the first boy's.

'No.' Ursula turned to the muddy boy. 'You were the first one to show me your knife. You were kind. You get the Venus, if you want it.'

The boy nodded eagerly and held out his belt. She handed over her Venus and strapped on the belt with the knife in its sheath.

The boys were crowding around the boy with the Venus, some slapping him on the back, others teasing him.

Ursula ignored them. 'Dear God of Jonathan, Lupus and Clio,' she prayed. 'I don't really know who you are, but you gave your son as a substitute for mankind. So please help me succeed in my plan.' Then she added 'Amen', as Jonathan always did.

'*Carpe diem!*' said Loquax fluttering down on to her shoulder.

'Not now, Loquax,' she cried and batted him away.

The boys all took a step back and the brown-skinned one made the Roman sign against evil.

'Hey there! You kids!' came an angry man's voice and they all turned to see half a dozen legionaries jogging towards them across the grass. 'Get away from our crane!' The man shouting must be an officer; he had two feathers either side of his helmet.

Heart pounding, Ursula turned to the boys. 'Wish me luck,' she said. She kicked off her sandals, took a few steps back and ran at the crane.

A leap took her up on to its surface. The wood beneath the soles of her feet was smooth but not slippery, straight-grained

207

and slightly pink. 'Dear Brother Ash Tree,' she whispered as she scrambled up its slope using hands as well as feet. 'Thank you for giving your life to make this crane. Help me do the same for the twins.'

For a moment it seemed she was back on board the merchant ship *Centaur*, whose ropes she could climb and down whose slippery mast she could slide.

She felt a huge confidence pour into her.

She could do this.

She could do this!

There were ropes every so often around the beam of the crane and each time she came to one she gripped it with her fingers and pulled hard, giving herself renewed momentum.

And now, miraculously, she was halfway up and had reached the place where the hook was attached to the beam. She hugged the beam and rested one foot in the hook so that she wouldn't slip back or fall off.

She saw that the hook was tied to the crane with a simple sailor's knot, easy to undo with one hand. She did not even need the knife. She laughed as she realised that what she had done was not really difficult. A soldier or slave must have done the same thing to lash the hook to the crane, and he would come back up in order to release it when they resumed work.

She settled her bare left foot into the supporting curve of the iron hook, feeling the cold rough metal as her friend, not her foe. For a brief moment she felt a huge surge of pride in being Roman. What miracles of engineering her race had accomplished! The crane was as strong as an oak and had not even trembled as she ran up it.

'Hey, you! Girl! Get down from there!'

She looked down and her stomach sank as she saw the tiny

upturned faces of soldiers and boys below.

She remembered something Juba had once said: 'A good death can make up for a bad life.'

'God of Jonathan,' she whispered, 'give me a good death. One like your son's. One not in vain. Help me save the twins.' Then she undid the simple knot, took a breath and pushed herself into space.

Chapter Fifty-One
MONTANUS

Fronto and Vindex had been assigned to protect Vegetus in case of another riot. Feelings were running high about the battle to the death between the beautiful twins.

He and Vindex stood right down on the arena, backs against the wall, armed with javelins as well as swords, daggers, bows and arrows. Bircha and Bouda had been tossing bread to the crowds and now came to stand beside them, for apart from the unfinished arch there were no visible exits down on the future racecourse.

For this reason, Fronto and Vindex and the two girls were able to hear every word the twins said to one another.

'Why couldn't you leave me be?' said the twin in the black loincloth, as he took the sword offered to him by Vegetus, who was also acting as referee. Fronto knew it was Raven because he spoke Latin with an accent.

'I thought you might be looking for me,' said Castor. The referee had to put the sword in his hand and close his fingers around the handle.

'I ran away from you!' cried Raven. 'Why would I want to find you?'

'To find out who you truly are.'

Vegetus stepped out of the circle drawn in the sand. 'Begin the battle!' he commanded in his huge voice.

'My mother was in the middle of telling me!' Raven circled his brother. 'Then men eager for your reward broke into our house and dragged me away!'

He swung his sword at Castor, who parried just in time.

'I'm sorry your foster mother didn't finish telling you,' said Castor. 'But do you at least admit you're of Roman and Jewish blood?'

'Maybe, but I hate you for what you did!' Once again he swung at Castor and this time sparks flew up when their swords clashed. The two were both crouching now as they circled each other.

'I thought you believed in peace and non-violence?' Castor grunted as he jumped back to avoid another swipe.

'I did. Until you killed my father!'

Raven began to swing one way, then jabbed his sword forward, taking Castor by surprise. His brother twisted just in time; the sword missed him by a finger's width.

'I didn't kill your father!' Castor swung back angrily. Sparks flew again as the swords clashed. 'He died trying to kill me . . . when he thought I was you!'

'What?' Raven's face was suddenly white as chalk.

'Yes!' Castor was panting. He let his sword arm hang loose. 'He put Bouda and me in a giant wicker man and was about to set us on fire. I was dressed as you and he didn't know I was your brother.'

'It's not true!' Raven charged Castor, who once again swivelled and let him pass by. Raven stumbled and fell on to one knee, but he was up a moment later and once again crouched in the ready position. 'My stepfather loved me and would never have harmed me.'

'He thought you betrayed him,' said Castor, 'because of a speech I gave. He turned on you without hesitation.'

'No! I don't believe it!'

'Yes, you do! You know it's true. You know how vengeful he was.'

'NO!' Raven swung and sparks flew.

'YES!' Castor was gasping for breath. 'But it doesn't matter . . . that he didn't love you . . . because he wasn't your real father!'

'He was the only father I ever knew!' Raven was weeping.

'But now you have a brother who would die for you!' Castor was also weeping.

The crowds were jeering, for they wanted more than a few swings of the sword. They wanted blood.

Fronto could see a man in the black mask of Charon advance with a red-hot poker. He knew that Polyphemus would be forced to prod the twins into action if they didn't begin to fight properly.

Castor must have noticed the red-hot poker, for he made a listless swipe in the direction of his brother.

Then, to Fronto's astonishment, he shouted a verse from the Aeneid, '*If Pollux could bring back his brother at the cost of his own life.*'

'What?' asked Raven.

'A quote from a great Roman poet named Virgil. If they must kill one of us, it should be me! All I ask is that you forgive me, brother, as I forgive you for what you're about to do.'

Castor tossed aside his sword and knelt on the sand. Then he closed his eyes and lifted his chin, and exposed his ivory-white neck to Raven's blade.

Chapter Fifty-Two
META

U rsula was flying.

A rush of air made her hair and feathered cape flap behind her as she swooped down and down on the end of a taut rope. Below her, people sitting on the north bank were looking up, their eyes and mouths making Os of surprise. Some of them ducked, as if she might hit them, but she didn't touch even a hair of their heads.

Now she was over the sandy part of the racetrack, missing the top of the pink marble meta by inches.

And now she was rising up above a rank of legionaries also gazing up at her in astonishment and now she was over the veterans on their wooden seats and big Montanus, his wet mouth an O like the others. The rope had twisted as she started the swing back down and now it turned back so that she could see the twins on the sand with Vegetus, the two soldiers and Charon all approaching.

Relief mixed with panic, for although she saw no blood, one of them was kneeling in the manner of a defeated gladiator bravely awaiting the death blow.

Soon she would be at the lowest part of her swing. That was when she should jump. But she was still so high!

'Lord, help me!' As she passed over the meta, she jumped.

For one breathless moment she hung in the air. Then the track leapt up to meet her and slammed the soles of her bare feet. The sand of the circus was firmer than the sand in the arena, and she cried out as her left ankle twisted beneath her.

The world tilted and for a moment it threatened to go dark as pain throbbed in her leg.

Then she was in full daylight again, on her hands and knees and looking up at Raven's face, which was full of wonder. Looking over her shoulder, she saw exactly the same expression on Castor's face.

She had to save them before Vegetus grabbed her or Charon poked her.

She scrambled to her feet and gasped at the pain in her ankle. But it only stopped her for a moment.

'My name is Ursula!' she shouted to the people, spreading her arms and making the feathered cape flutter.

The crowd fell silent, and out of the corner of her eye she saw Vegetus hold up his right hand, palm forward, to stop the advance of Charon and his red-hot poker.

She took a lungful of air. 'These brothers are fighting here today because of me, because I had a foolish idea!' She was speaking in Brittonic but suddenly remembered where she was. In Latin she said, 'It's my fault that these twins are here. I deserve to die, not one of them.'

'Ursula!' She heard Fronto's cry and caught a glimpse of armour from the corner of her eye. 'What are you doing?'

From the stands a few other people cried, 'No!' She thought one of the voices sounded like Prasutus.

But she fixed her gaze on Montanus. 'Gaius Curtius Montanus,' she said, 'our Princeps Domitian has given to you the power of life or death. Please don't kill these brothers who have only just come together after more than a dozen years of being apart! I offer my life instead.'

Then she knelt on the sand beside Castor and bowed her head.

Everything was silent apart from the cries of seagulls overhead. The silence stretched on, and when she glanced up from under her eyebrows she saw Montanus conferring with an important-looking soldier.

'Hurry up!' she muttered to herself. 'Do it before I lose my nerve and try to run away!'

'Ursula, what are you doing?' came Castor's urgent whisper. 'I already offered to die instead of Raven.'

Ursula looked at Castor, still on his knees beside her.

'You offered your life for Raven?'

He nodded, his grey eyes wide.

Ursula felt an irrational surge of joy. 'And I'm offering my life for you! So the two of you can be together.'

Suddenly there was a thump in the sand next to her and Prasutus was there, somersaulting forwards.

'Don't kill the girl,' he cried. 'Kill me!'

'Prasutus!' Ursula said. 'Where did you come from?'

He gripped her shoulders and raised her up. 'Same place you did,' he said under his breath. 'I jumped up and caught the hook as it swung over me. Now stand back and be quiet!' He knelt where she had been kneeling a moment before.

'No!' cried Ursula, kneeling again. 'I couldn't bear it if you died instead of me!'

'This is quite extraordinary!' came Montanus's voice from above. 'I have never heard of such a thing happening. I am most impressed at the noble offers of self-sacrifice from the Roman boy, the African girl and the British youth. Stand up to receive my judgement!'

The three of them rose, trembling, to their feet, waiting to hear Montanus's verdict.

'Your quote from Virgil touched me deeply!' said Montanus to Castor. 'And your willingness to offer your life even more so. I declare you and your brother both free!'

For a heartbeat, the thousands of spectators were silent. Then they erupted into ecstatic cheers.

Castor and Raven looked at one another, then Raven threw aside his sword and embraced his brother.

Impossibly, the cheers grew even louder.

When at long last they died down, Montanus turned to Ursula and Prasutus. 'For your bravery,' he said, 'I declare the two of you free also.'

Ursula felt her spirit soar and tears of happiness blurred her eyes. They were all free!

'However!' blared Montanus. 'The gods and the crowd will have their blood. Although these beautiful youths are now free, I command them to fight the beasts with nothing but their swords.'

As the crowd cheered, Montanus gestured to a pair of soldiers. 'Take the girl and the Briton to the Praetorium. I want to question them after these games have finished.' Then he looked at Charon, who still stood with his cooling poker. 'Do you have any beasts?'

'Only the deer, a bear and a hound.' The boyish voice that came from behind Charon's mask belonged to Polyphemus.

Montanus nodded. 'Then let the twins fight bear and hound,' he said. 'As soon as these two are out of the way, release them!'

Vegetus added, 'And prod them with the poker if necessary.'

'No!' screamed Ursula. 'Not Gartha! Not Big Ursula!'

One of the soldiers put his hand on her arm. She shoved against him, but he was as solid as the pink cone of marble behind him. He gripped her arm and pulled it back, and with a quick movement bound her wrists behind her.

'No!' Ursula was crying. 'Please don't make them fight the dog and the bear. The twins will kill them!'

Half blinded by tears, she let the soldier push her forward out of the hippodrome, under the unfinished arch of the racecourse and up the deserted road towards the town walls. As she limped miserably up the road, Prasutus walked beside her, and she saw that his face was full of anguish, too.

Suddenly, one of the soldiers marching beside her uttered an oath of surprise as Loquax fluttered down on to her shoulder. Although Loquax was silent, the two soldiers made the sign against evil.

Behind them, a roar rose from the circus and she knew that Polyphemus had released Ursula and Gartha. In one way she was glad she could not see what was happening, as cheers, shouts and gasps followed them up the road. Once she thought she heard music but could not be certain for a huge roar drowned it out a few moments later. As they passed through the south gate of Camulodunum, Ursula knew the bear and hound she loved were gone forever.

Chapter Fifty-Three
MULSUM

Ursula sat shivering, her wrists still bound behind her.

'Please untie the girl,' Prasutus begged the soldiers. Neither soldier responded so he added, 'She won't run away.' Ursula felt him gazing at her. 'Will you?'

But she was too wretched to answer.

She heard the scuff of hobnail boots on marble as one of the legionaries moved behind her.

She felt her cormorant-feather cape shift on her shoulders, a brief tightening of the binding on her wrists, and suddenly her arms were free. The soldier must have cut the leather thongs that had bound them.

'Thank you,' said Prasutus to the soldier. He put his arm round Ursula's shoulders, causing Loquax to fly up on to the bracket of a hanging oil lamp and ask, '*What ARE you doing?*'

Both soldiers clanked as they made the sign against evil and exchanged nervous glances.

'What an extraordinary afternoon!' came a cultured man's deep voice, and a moment later an officer in a plumed helmet entered the courtyard. 'I have never seen anything like it. The Emperor will be hugely pleased, I'm sure.'

'I hope so!' puffed Montanus, following him in with a flutter of his broad-striped toga. 'It was certainly unorthodox!'

'Greetings, brave children,' the officer addressed Ursula and Prasutus. 'Sit, please sit!' He gestured towards a cushioned bench between two of the columns. 'And you, too, dear Quintus. Take my best leather armchair.'

'Thank you, legate!' The bronze and leather armchair creaked as Montanus lowered his toga-wrapped bulk into it.

Ursula's stomach was beating like her heart. 'What happened?' she asked. 'Are they . . . ?'

The legate held out his arms, like a slave being crucified on a cross.

At first Ursula didn't understand. Then, as two slave boys rushed forward, she realised the gesture was not meant for her. One boy undid the toggles on one side of the legate's bronze breastplate, opened it like an oyster shell and placed it on a nearby chest. The other boy removed his cloak.

'Don't worry,' said the legate to Ursula, as the boys went to stand by the wall. 'The twins are fine. And so are the beasts. Even after prodding they seemed reluctant to fight, and when the flower girl started playing her flute and they began to dance together, Montanus here had no choice but to spare them, too.'

Ursula stared at him for a moment, then clapped her hands and squealed. 'Gartha and Big Ursula are alive? Bircha saved them by playing her flute?'

'Yes!' Montanus gave a wheezing laugh. 'I had to spare everyone! Thank goodness one of the gladiators died,' he added, 'though he will be most expensive to replace . . .'

Ursula's smile faded at this, but she could not suppress her joy at Gartha's survival.

The legate snapped his fingers at the waiting slave boys. 'Bring mulsum and nuts. Enough for four.' Then he turned to

Ursula. 'Tell me.' He removed his white-plumed helmet and set it beside the gold-coloured breastplate. 'What is your name and where are you from?'

'My name is Ursula,' she said happily. 'I'm from Rome.'

She felt Prasutus stiffen and give her a warning squeeze, but she was too relieved to care.

'My name is Prasutus,' said Prasutus quickly. 'I come from the Iceni tribe.'

One the slave boys came back into the room with silver cups on a silver tray. All four goblets contained the same wine, a sweet mulsum with dates, honey, saffron and a peppery aftertaste. It was so delicious that she drained her cup and held it out for more. The slave boy refilled her cup. The other boy placed a big silver bowl of nuts on a citrus-wood table between Montanus and the legate, and a smaller bowl between her and Prasutus on the bench. Ursula dug in, suddenly ravenous. The twins were alive! And Bircha's flute had saved Gartha and Ursula! 'Thank you, God of Jonathan!' she whispered.

'What did you just say?' The legate was leaning forward in his chair. The garden was behind her and his face was lit by early afternoon light. He had warm brown eyes that reminded her of Doctor Jonathan's.

'I was just saying thank you for the refreshments!' she lied. 'They're delicious.'

Montanus grunted his agreement as he tossed another handful of nuts into his own mouth.

The legate was about to say something when Loquax flew down to the citrus-wood table and cocked his head at the bowl. '*Carpe diem!*' said the bird.

'Great Jupiter's eyebrows!' exclaimed the legate. 'A talking bird! Is it yours?'

Ursula nodded, her mouth full of nuts.

'I've only encountered one like that once before.' The legate leaned back in his chair and frowned up at the coffered ceiling. 'Now, where was that?'

'Somewhere in Rome?' said Montanus, his mouth also full.

'Perhaps . . .' The legate put down his cup, took an almond from the bowl and held it out to Loquax on the palm of his hand.

'*Carpe diem!*' repeated Loquax, daintily taking the nut. He tossed back his little yellow-capped head to swallow it. '*Ave, Domitian!*'

The legate's face brightened. '*That's* where I last saw a bird like that! On the Palatine Hill! It was a favourite pet of the Emperor Domitian.'

'You're right!' said Montanus, spraying bits of nut. 'Our Princeps had a bird just like that one. It came from a faraway land and was worth as much as an educated Greek slave . . .' Suddenly, a strange expression passed over his face and he heaved himself out of his chair. He was staring, bug-eyed, at Ursula.

Her heart began to thud. *Oh no!* she thought. *Have I said something that might put Fronto and Juba in danger? Montanus knows the Emperor is after us. He'll turn us in and get the reward!*

But instead of accusing Ursula, the big man turned to the legate. 'Do you have a latrine? I need it most urgently.'

'Of course. I have a four-seater in my small bathhouse.' The legate snapped his fingers and when the one of slave boys stepped forward he said, 'Show our honoured guest to the latrines, Puer. Make sure there are some clean sponge-sticks,' he added.

'*Carpe diem!*' called Loquax as Montanus rushed from the room.

The legate swirled his wine and stared thoughtfully into the

221

silver cup. 'You know,' he said, 'I was with the Emperor shortly after his talking bird flew away. He was bereft. That was about two years ago . . . Where did you say you bought that bird?'

Ursula's skin prickled and the little hairs on the back of her neck lifted up.

Two years ago Loquax had flown into one of the marble discs that hung between the columns of the Rose Courtyard of her family's Roman townhouse. Their Roman townhouse was on the Palatine Hill, within a stone's throw of the imperial palace.

Could Loquax have been the Emperor's special pet?

Prasutus came to her rescue. 'Didn't you tell me you bought the bird in the port of Ostia?'

'Yes!' Ursula shot him a grateful look. 'My father bought him three years ago for my seventh birthday.'

The legate raised his eyebrow. 'You are only ten? How did you come to be in Britannia? Swinging like a monkey from a polyspaston? Offering your life to save those two beautiful youths?'

Ursula's mind was frozen, like a fawn caught in the gaze of a wolf.

'Tell me,' he said, leaning forward once again. 'Were you perhaps inspired by the teaching of the philosopher Arepo?'

'Arepo?' The name was familiar but for a moment she couldn't think from where.

Then she remembered. It was from Lupus's puzzle square, the nonsense name. It was the code name for Jesus, the Jewish prophet who had come to rid the world of animal sacrifices once and for all.

'Arepo!' she exclaimed. 'Yes, I am a follower of his philosophy.'

The legate nodded. 'I suspected as much. My wife admires his teaching. She sometimes speaks of another kingdom, but a spiritual kingdom rather than an earthly kingdom.' He drained his wine and put the silver cup on the citrus-wood table. 'I will give you the same advice I give her,' he said. 'Be very careful when you talk about such things. Do them in secret and not in public.'

He stood up. 'Now, return to your friends and be on your way. Quickly, before Montanus returns. And may your God bless you, prosper you and keep you safe.'

Chapter Fifty-Four
BAPTISMA

Ursula's ankle still hurt, but when the sight of the pantomime wagon came into view she limped as fast as she could.

They were all gathered around something.

'Gartha!' she cried, as she came into the circle of wagons. They all looked up and Gartha emerged from their midst and limped towards Ursula.

'Oh no! What happened to her?' cried Ursula, throwing her arms round the dog's woolly neck.

'I'm afraid she was burned,' said Doctor Jonathan. 'I was just putting ointment on the wounds.'

'I had to poke her three times,' said Polyphemus, his face wet with tears. 'But she still wouldn't attack them.'

'Nor would the bear,' said Fronto.

'And then I couldn't stand it any more!' cried Bircha. 'So I pulled out my flute and played the dancing song.'

'I've never seen such bravery,' said Fronto, and put his arm round her.

Ursula stood up and stared in amazement. *Her brother Fronto liked Bircha!*

'I clapped the rhythm with my hands,' said Bouda.

'Because I wasn't there,' Bolianus said.

Juba put his arms round Ursula. 'You were so brave,' he said. 'You will make a wonderful Stoic.'

Ursula shook her head. 'I'm a follower of the Way, now,' she said happily. 'Like Doctor Jonathan!'

Juba looked stunned but Lupus and Clio cheered and came forward to hug her, too.

'*Meeer!*' said Meer, not to be outdone, and she rubbed herself back and forth against their legs.

'*Find Jonathan!*' said Loquax.

'Here I am,' said Doctor Jonathan with a rare smile.

Someone was missing. Two people, in fact. 'Where are the twins?' she asked.

'Right there,' said Bouda. 'In the shade of that oak tree.'

She pointed at Castor and Raven, standing face-to-face at the edge of the woods. They were deep in conversation and holding hands.

'Great Juno's beard!' exclaimed Ursula. 'They look like they're in love!' Then she clapped her hand over her mouth.

Everyone laughed and looked at the twins.

'They probably are a little bit in love,' said Prasutus.

Bolianus nodded. 'Imagine being that handsome and meeting your exact copy, but raised in a completely different world and culture.'

'They're like the myth of Narcissus,' offered Vindex, 'if his reflection was real.'

'But they hated each other at first,' said Ursula.

Juba cocked his head. 'Put yourself in their place,' he said, 'as we Stoics are encouraged to do. Imagine this. What if you or I could go back and meet ourselves a year ago, when we first escaped from Rome. Remember how flabby and spoiled we were?'

Ursula gave a bitter laugh. 'You're right. British me would despise Roman me.'

'No!' said Prasutus.

'Yes!' said Ursula. 'Just like British Popo despised Roman Soso!'

'But now you're different, aren't you?' said Doctor Jonathan.

Lupus held up his wax tablet. BORN OF THE SPIRIT.

'Yes, I feel fresh and new!' said Ursula. 'Like I died and came back!'

'That's what baptism symbolises,' said Jonathan. 'Death to our old natures and rebirth to a new one.'

Ursula saw her brothers exchange a glance. 'Don't worry,' she heard Juba whisper to Fronto. 'It won't last. She changes religions as often as she changes her tunic.'

Ursula was about to protest but instead she closed her eyes and whispered a prayer. 'Please Lord, help me be steadfast in my new-found faith.'

'Look!' cried Clio. 'There's a stream. We should baptise her right now!'

Half an hour later, dressed in a brand new nettle-cloth undertunic, with Lupus and Clio holding her and Jonathan saying the words, they pressed her down into the water.

And when she resurfaced she felt the surge of pure love and clarity she felt before a seizure.

'Lord!' She lifted her dripping face to the sun. 'If a seizure is the price then I am willing to pay it.'

But the convulsions never came, and they feasted long into the night.

Chapter Fifty-Five
DISCIPULA

They found out the next day that Montanus was already on his way back to Rome. He had hastily boarded a ship at Camulodunum, said Vegetus, taking only his two slaves with him, and leaving his steward to tie up loose ends.

Vegetus gave them their pay. Even Fronto and Vindex received a gold coin, though their regular salary came from an army strongbox.

The surviving gladiators were sold as a job lot to the legate at Camulodunum along with Polyphemus, Big Ursula and the two tame deer.

Somehow, Ursula knew the legate would look after all of them.

So it was a much smaller convoy than usual making its way southwest to Londinium on the last day of the month named after Julius Caesar.

Ursula was sitting cross-legged on the floor of the carruca with Gartha crouching sphinx-like beside her. Gartha's burns needed at least another day of rest to heal completely.

It was a bright summer morning and the carruca door was open, allowing them to look back the way they had come.

'It's strange facing this direction,' she said to Doctor Jonathan, who was sitting behind her in Lupus's folding chair.

'Some philosophers claim that this is how the Greeks see time,' came his reply. 'The things that have just passed, that is to say happened, are still in view and we can describe them well. But the things that happened a few weeks, months or years ago are now far behind us on the distant horizons of our minds.'

Ursula pondered this for a moment, then shook her head. 'Not for me,' she said. 'My memories are more like frescoes on a wall lit by flashes of lightning.'

'Excellent description,' said Jonathan. He paused. 'How does it feel to have a new God living inside you?'

'Everything seems fresh and clean,' said Ursula. 'But I keep wanting to cry at the smallest things.'

'That will pass,' said Jonathan. 'But it is a sign that something inside you has changed and softened. What will you do now?' he asked her.

'What do you mean?'

'Has God called you? He always calls you to do things for him: good deeds that will bring you joy and fulfilment. These are the things he created you to do.'

Ursula twisted to look back up at him. 'God created me?'

'That's what the followers of Moses and Jesus believe.' He smiled down at her and said, 'That God wove you in your mother's womb, and that he has a plan for each of us.'

Ursula pondered this for a moment, as she stroked Gartha. It was both wonderful and daunting to think that God had created her with a purpose in mind. She closed her eyes. 'Lord,' she whispered, 'what is your purpose for me?'

She had barely formed the words when an image dropped into her heart. It was so clear that it made her gasp.

'What?' She heard the amusement in his voice.

'Doctor Jonathan, are there animal doctors?'

'Of course. Animals are worth a great deal to those who use them, whether it is the ox behind the plough or the mule circling a millstone at the bakery. It is in their owners' interest to keep the animals as healthy and happy as possible. Tell me,' he said, 'did that thought just drop into your mind?'

She nodded. 'I don't know where it came from. I never thought of being a doctor before. Especially not an animal doctor.'

'It came from God,' he said. 'Your eternal soul within you, which God also created, knows what it was made for.'

'So God created me to be an animal doctor?'

'Very probably. But he didn't make you for just one thing. He created you to do a thousand things, both big and small.'

'But also to be an animal doctor.'

'Yes. Perhaps to be an animal doctor.'

Ursula had a sudden revelation.

'Last month,' she said, 'when Fronto came to Mistletoe Oak and told us we had to find a doctor named Jonathan ben Mordecai, it was the last thing I wanted to do. But God knew that of all the people in the world, you were the best person for me to find. And not just because you have information that can defeat our enemy.'

'That information won't become important for another year,' he said. 'In the meantime I'm going to keep a low profile and heal the sick, which is what I've been doing for the past dozen years, anyway.'

They were passing through silver birch woods. The white trunks and trembling green leaves filled Ursula with joy. Gartha's nose twitched and she raised her head to catch an interesting smell.

As Ursula stroked the old scent-hound, she suddenly saw that the world was beautiful but fallen, just as Jonathan had once said. But she could help. She could mend and comfort the creatures who had no words and could only plead with their eyes. From the tiniest sparrow to the biggest ox.

One day she would marry and have children, but not for many years, and in the meantime she would travel with this sad doctor who had so much to teach her.

Without turning to look at him, she made an announcement. 'Doctor Jonathan,' she said. 'I am going to travel with you and be your apprentice.'

'Really?'

'Really!' she said briskly. 'You are going to teach me all you know and I will help you be happy again.'

She turned to see his reaction. His eyes were fixed on the road as it unscrolled behind them.

She expected him to protest, but he merely nodded.

'Just the other day,' he said, 'God told me exactly the same thing.'

And she saw that his eyes were full of tears.

FINIS

WHAT THE LATIN CHAPTER
HEADERS MEAN

1. LUCUS – sacred grove
   A wood, glade or thicket of trees sacred to a deity.

2. CASUS – a falling down
   A tumble, fall or overthrow.

3. PISTILLUM – pestle
   Cylinder of stone or marble with a rounded end, used to grind things such as herbs and spices in a bowl called a mortarium or mortar.

4. MUS – mouse
   The Latin word used for several species of rodent, possibly including rats.

5. SCIRPI – bulrushes
   A kind of light river reed which was used for baskets, mats or for spreading over the ground as a floor covering.

6. FELES – cat
   We get the word 'feline' from the Latin word for cat.

7. AVIS – bird
   We get the word 'aviary' from the Latin word for bird.

8. VENEFICIUM – poisoning
   The word for poisoning is also the Latin word for sorcery, magic or the preparation of magic potions. Kids, do NOT try to make any of these potions at home!

9,   BENEFICIARII – special agents
Beneficiarii consularis were soldiers of the governor, detached on special duties.

10. LEGATIO – mission
Literally 'a delegation' but it came to mean any mission where chosen representatives are sent on a quest.

11. RECUSATIO – a refusal
The word can also mean a counter-argument or defence.

12. CONVULSIO – a seizure
We get the English word 'convulsion' from this word.

13. CARRUCA – travelling carriage
A four-wheeled travelling coach. It is linked to the words 'carry' and 'carriage'.

14. PANTOMIMUS – pantomime dancer
A Roman pantomime was like a ballet-dancer who used his body to act out a story sung by a troupe of musicians.

15. LINGUA – tongue
We get the word 'linguistics', the study of language, from the Latin word for tongue or language.

16. GREX – troupe
Literally a 'flock, herd or swarm' the word could also apply to a group of people in a band or company.

17. RIVUS – stream
We get the words 'river' and 'rivulet' the Latin for a small stream of water or a brook.

18. PHILOSOPHUS – philosopher
    The first Christian apostles might have been mistaken for philosophers. NB Theophorus of Antioch is invented.

19. VIROCONIUM – Wroxeter
    Troops had moved on from the fortress at Wroxeter around five years before this story takes place, but there was still a thriving settlement there.

20. BESTIAE – wild beasts
    A common punishment for criminals and rebels in Roman times was to have them thrown ad bestias – to the wild beasts – during a public show.

21. LUPUS – wolf
    We get the word 'lupine' from the Latin word for wolf.

22. DAMA – deer
    Fallow deer were introduced to Britain by the Romans in the first century.

23. URSA – bear
    The name Ursula is a diminutive of the Latin word for bear, so means 'little bear'.

24. SEGOSA – scent hound
    A rare word found in only a few places, including Vindolanda, it seems to mean a type of bloodhound. This is the feminine version for a female dog.

25. DEVA – Chester
    Deva was an important legionary fortress and settlement on the site of the modern city of Chester.

26. DEFECTIO – rebellion
We get the word 'defect' from the Latin word for desertion or revolt.

27. CHRISTIANUS – Christian
The Christian scriptures were not in place at this time and the teachings of many who called themselves Christians would seem very strange to us today.

28. ARENA – sandy space
The word comes from the word harena or 'sand' and originally meant a place where men fought other men or beasts.

29. CONFESSIO – confession
The word could mean a statement of belief as much as a confession of guilt.

30. TEMO – pole
This was the beam that ran from the body of a wagon, plough or chariot to the yoke across the necks of the animals pulling it.

31. SAL – salt
We get the word 'salary' from salt, it was originally the amount of money given to a Roman soldier to buy salt.

32. MAMUCIUM – Manchester
Mamucium, near the modern city of Manchester, was originally the site of an auxiliary fort.

33. IUDAEUS – Jew
Jews were often confused with Christians from the time of Jesus on, because many of the first Christians had been born Jews.

34. PHILOTIMIA – love of honour
   The love of honour (and fear of humiliation) was a powerful motivation for men's actions in the world of Ancient Greece and Rome.

35. URTICAE – nettles
   Cloth made of the stem fibres of nettles was considered apotropaic, i.e. able to turn away bad luck.

36. RES ILLICITAE – banned objects
   These were items usually associated with an illegal or forbidden religion.

37. EBORACUM – York
   Eboracum was a legionary fortress and settlement on the site of the modern city of York.

38. ADVENTUS – arrival
   We get the word 'advent' from the Latin word for arrival.

39. VINUM – wine
   We get the word 'vine' from the Latin word for wine.

40. FABULA – story
   We get the word 'fable' from the Latin word for story.

41. SALTATIO – dance
   Nobody knows exactly what ancient Roman dance or pantomime looked like.

42. FEBRIS – fever
   In Roman times, doctor gave fevers names based on their frequency of occurrence, which tells us that many were probably malarial.

43. CAMULODUNUM – Colchester
One of the towns destroyed by Boudica around AD 60, by AD 95 Camulodunum was an important city again.

44. DIVINATIO - prophecy
Romans tried to predict the future, or the gods' approval of a future event, in many ways.

45. BASILICA – law court
Almost every Roman city had a large hall in which legal cases could be heard.

46. SCAENA – backdrop
The word literally means the backdrop behind the stage of a theatre, but by extension can also mean the stage or the theatre itself.

47. CIRCUS – circle
In Roman times, the word usually meant a hippodrome or racecourse. Most scholars believe the Colchester hippodrome was built at least 20 years after the events of this book, but at the time of writing we have no firm evidence either way.

48. SACRIFICIUM – sacrifice
Animal sacrifice was a daily part of life in Rome and the Roman provinces. It was seen as a way of keeping the gods' good will.

49. SPECTACULUM – public show
We get the word 'spectacle' from the Latin word.

50. POLYSPASTON – crane
Romans were clever engineers and developed ways to lift huge blocks of marble and other stone.

51. MONTANUS – mountainous
The word refers to mountains but was also the name of one of Domitian's advisors. There is no evidence that Montanus ever came to Britain.

52. META – turning-post
The Latin word means 'boundary mark' or 'goal' but also the conical turning-posts of a racecourse.

53. MULSUM – honeyed-wine
A popular Roman drink of honey and spices mixed into wine. It was sometimes served warm or even hot, like mulled wine.

54. BAPTISMA – baptism
The Latin word comes from the Greek word for dipping under or washing.

55. DISCIPULA – apprentice
The root of the word means 'learn', so it can also mean any kind of female learner, a scholar, a student or a disciple. The masculine is discipulus.

Read on for a sneak peek of the next book in
The Roman Quests, *Return to Rome* . . .

The little girl in the tartan tunic was running for her life.

Six-year-old Bouda was the youngest cutpurse in Tyranus's gang. She often had to flee the people she robbed. But on this foggy winter day in the docks of Londinium she was running from two Roman soldiers.

Their hobnail boots clattered on the wooden wharf as they chased her around oak barrels of beer from Germania, past amphoras of olive oil from Galatia and between crates of Samian ware from Gaul. At least barefoot Bouda had the advantage of knowing the docks of Londinium like a rabbit knows its warren. But the soldiers were bigger and faster.

What would they do with her when they caught her? Would they beat her? Imprison her? Crucify her?

Her heart was thumping like a rabbit's and her red hair flew out behind her.

Bouda was proud of her hair and liked to leave it unpinned. Tyranus said it was like a flame in the fog.

It was foggy now and in a world of white, her shining copper locks might get her killed.

Behind her, a clatter of armour told her one of the soldiers had slipped and fallen onto the wet planks.

As the other soldier stopped to help him, Bouda darted underneath an unhitched wagon.

Crouching in the dim light, she shrank back against one of the wheels and waited for the soldiers to run past. But instead of running on, they stopped right beside her hiding place.

She could see the hems of their red woollen tunics, their bare legs, their boots and the tips of their swords.

'Jupiter's eyebrows!' panted the one with hairy calves. 'Where's she gone?'

'I think she went into that warehouse,' gasped the one with the bumpy knees.

'Impossible! It's too far away and the door is closed. She was right in front of me, almost within arm's reach!'

'Why are we chasing a little girl anyway?' The wagon creaked as one of the soldiers leant against it. 'I mean, I know she runs with that gang of cutpurses, but it's not our job to save every fool who comes off the boat. It's humiliating.'

'What's humiliating is that she got away,' muttered his companion. Then he lowered his voice even further. 'There's a rumour she's Boudica's great granddaughter.'

Underneath the wagon the little girl's eyes grew wide with wonder. Her boss Tyranus often told her she was descended from the famous red-haired warrior queen named Boudica. But whenever she told the older boys they never believed her.

'Boudica's granddaughter? Hah!' scoffed the soldier with bumpy knees. 'I'll bet they say that about every red-headed girl here in Britannia.'

'Apparently this one is legitimate. She wears the ring of a Roman legionary of the Second Augusta.'

Beneath the wagon, little Bouda held out her left hand and looked at the ring on her thumb. The stone was the same reddish orange as her hair. Carved into it was a tiny creature with a goat's body and a fish's tail: a capricorn. Did it really prove she was Boudica's descendant?

'Even if she is Boudica's granddaughter, why does the governor want her?'

'It's not the governor who wants her. It's Domitian.'

Bouda's green eyes grew wider. Domitian was the emperor of Rome. Everybody knew that.

'It's been nearly forty years since Boudica burned Londinium,' said Bumpy Knees. 'And look how it's risen from the ashes. Nobody cares about Boudica anymore, much less her great granddaughter.'

'Domitian does. He hasn't been doing very well in his wars recently. He needs a good triumph.'

'And you think a little girl will do it for him?'

'Yeah. I reckon he'll parade her through the streets of Rome and then publicly execute her.'

Bouda's throat was suddenly dry. She wasn't sure what 'execute' meant but it didn't sound good.

She shrank back against the wooden wheel of the cart.

Suddenly an arm darted through the spokes and hooked her waist. Before she could scream, a cold hand clamped over her mouth.

After a moment of pure terror she relaxed. It was a boy's hand. She knew it belonged to Ferox, the nine-year-old leader of the gang she had been assigned to. He must have been looking for her all this time.

Being caught by Ferox was almost as bad as being captured by soldiers. For a mad moment Bouda considered biting his hand and screaming to the soldiers for help. But they were already moving away, so she let herself go limp.

When the two legionaries were gone, Ferox dragged her out from under the wagon. 'Where were you? Did you get any purses?'

When Bouda refused to answer he reached down the front of her tunic and found two money pouches. She had cut their strings with the small folding knife tied around her wrist.

Smirking, he took the pouches and when she glared at him he pinched her bare arms to make her squeal. But Bouda refused to make a sound. Even when he slapped her face she remained stubbornly silent.

In disgust, Ferox grabbed her wrist and dragged her along the wharf, back between crates, amphoras and barrels and finally up dark wooden stairs to the second floor of a nearby warehouse. Tyranus sat behind a table laden with items from the morning's haul. He was examining the carving in a signet ring.

'Bouda nearly got caught by two Roman soldiers,' said Ferox, still gripping her arm so hard that it hurt. 'They think she's Boudica's great granddaughter. They were talking about sending her to Domitian to be in some big parade.'

The boss of the East End Gang got up from the table, came round and squatted down so that his head was level with hers. Tyranus had large dark eyes with long eyelashes and would have been good-looking if not for the scar across his nose. 'You know what Domitian does to little girls,' he said in a voice as soft as velvet. 'He does horrible things. And then he eats them.'

Bouda stared back at him, her mouth clamped shut, and nodded. She was determined not to cry.

Tyranus stood up and shook his head. He glanced at Ferox. 'Did she at least cut a purse or two?'

'No,' Ferox lied. He released his grip on Bouda and pulled out three pouches. They included the two he had found down the front of her tunic. 'I got these, but she's useless.' He spat onto Bouda's bare foot. She managed not to flinch.

'Don't be so hard on the girl,' said Tyranus, emptying the contents of the purses onto the table. 'She is only six. Still…' He picked up a thin rod made of birch and turned to Bouda. 'You know the rules,' he said. 'If you come back empty-handed, you get the rod.'

Bouda nodded, shot Ferox a glare and then grinned. She brought her right hand to her mouth and spat out the pearl she had been holding in her cheek for nearly an hour.

It was covered with saliva but that only made it gleam more.

'Well, well, well.' Tyranus put down the rod and took the pearl. 'Look at that. The best tribute I've had all week. You did well, my little flame.' He patted Bouda's head. 'Tonight you'll get a slice of bread and honey as your reward, and you can sleep nearest the brazier.'

Ferox gave her a filthy look as she followed him out, but Bouda didn't care. She felt her heart swell with happiness. Tyranus was proud of her!

'Remember, Bouda,' Tyranus called after them. 'Gold and gems and pearls are the only things that will keep you safe in this world.'

Later that night, huddled on the sleeping mat with the other girls, Bouda was content. But what made her happy and warm was not the bread and honey in her stomach or the place nearest the brazier, but the memory of Tyranus's look of pride and his words of praise. They warmed her more than any coals in a bronze tripod.

'Gold and gems and pearls,' she whispered, 'are the only things that will keep me safe in this world.'